1/10

A NOVEL

PANAMA

by Shelby Hiatt

Houghton Mifflin
Houghton Mifflin Harcourt
Boston New York 2009

Houghton Mifflin is an imprint of
Houghton Mifflin Harcourt Publishing Company.

www.hmhbooks.com

The text of this book is set in Adobe Garamond.

Library of Congress Cataloging-in-Publication Data is on file.
ISBN 978-0-547-19600-8

Manufactured in the United States of America
MP 10 9 8 7 6 5 4 3 2 1

For Darren and Brett

THE ISTHMUS

One

1913. PANAMA. 3 P.M. A SWELTERING CLASSROOM.

Mrs. Ewing's Friday reminder: "Put your books away. Don't leave anything on top of your desk." She claps to get our attention but it's not necessary. We go through this every week. "Oil gangs coming tonight," she says.

But the oil gangs won't come inside tonight—they're for standing water and mosquito larvae around the building. Mrs. Ewing has an idea the air absorbs trace amounts of oil that seep inside and cover everything with a film—we have to clear our desks.

I shove everything in with my notebooks. I squeeze my pens and pencils together and jam them back, pay no attention to order or torn paper. I used to care about that kind of thing, no longer. I'll soon be at the cabin and none of this matters.

Minutes later the whole class, more than thirty of us, rides on the train that takes us home. Swift and efficient, the Canal Commission Railroad trundles beside the Cut, rocking, swaying, tunneling through sultry afternoon air toward Culebra. I keep a dreamy eye on everything—the gorge outside and the hijinks in the passenger car.

Alan carefully places his banana peel on the hat of a man sitting in front of us—Alan is the class comic. The man must be a tourist, because he wears a felt fedora with a brim and a crease in the top that perfectly cradles the banana peel. We stifle our laughter.

The man never moves, only reads his *Canal Record*. The other passengers don't notice, and in a few minutes he gets off at Barbacoas with the peel still in place. It's truly comical. Chalk one up for Alan—a man carrying a newspaper and briefcase with a banana peel on his hat. The man passes our window, the peel at eye level, and we fold with laughter.

Out on the platform people begin to notice. A kid points and his mother lowers his hand but she's smiling, and other heads turn and there are sniggers. The man grows uncomfortable and confused. Inside the train we're howling. We've cut loose, although my version of cutting loose is a languid, bemused look that I float out from my remote world.

The Barbacoas stop is short. The train pulls away and the man is still walking straight and stiff as though he's in Cincinnati, wondering why people are staring.

But this is not Cincinnati. This is the Canal Zone, and I'm enjoying this prank as much as the others. I'm part of the student mob and in two more stops I'll be getting off. There'll be no laughing at me. I'm one of them and insulated from their pranks, though it wouldn't bother me if I weren't. That's because I'm insulated in my private world from everything and this is the stop closest to the cabin where Federico lives. He's waiting for me and we'll spend two erotic hours together.

Nobody knows about this, not even the students, or I'd be their reigning queen, something that might have mattered to me some time ago but not now. Federico's waiting.

While they are laughing at a man with a banana peel in his hat, I'm amused because I have a secret that is much more interesting than their juvenile caper.

This is the best time of my life and these are the best kids I know, and in the flashing Panama sun I can't imagine it will ever end.

THE MIDWEST

Two

TEN YEARS EARLIER. DAYTON, OHIO.

We live next door to Wilbur and Orville Wright. (They have to live somewhere.)

They're a nice family: Carrie, the housekeeper; their sister, Katharine; and Milton, their father, who's called the Bishop. It's a position he has in the United Brethren Church—he's not the head of a diocese. But he is serious and scares the bejesus out of me, he's so humorless and proper. We're regular small-town citizens. Everybody calls Wil and Orville "the boys" and knows they're working on a flying machine, but it's nothing special. It's what they do, tinker and putter all day—they've been at it for years.

Two older brothers live on their own, and since their mother died they're a family of five. They're in the house next to us on Hawthorne Street, and since we are only three—Mother, Father, me—the Wright boys are like my brothers.

They work at their shop on Third Street or in the shed out

back and they let me help. I hand them tools and it makes me feel important. That's my earliest sense of self, being useful, and it's a nice feeling. So I'm pretty happy most of the time. Actually, I'm energetic and exuberant. I climb trees, build things, pattern myself after the boys as best I can.

They need starch boxes because they're the right size to make a model wind tunnel. I run home, empty Mother's starch into a mixing bowl, and bring back the box. Carrie empties hers and I deliver both boxes to the shed. I watch Orville and Wil put together the first wind tunnel and I think, *With help like that you can do most anything.* I absolutely believe it. I really am innocent. So is everyone around me.

I don't want to play dolls with Rosie Fisher down the street. She's Catholic, which is all right, but she goes to Catholic school with different friends and eight brothers and sisters. She's not in my world. She seems like a foreigner, and anyway, I'm not interested in dolls. I prefer the boys and their gizmos and half-built wings and spokes and gears hanging on the wall.

When I stay for supper at the Wrights', they say grace, then talk about work: ". . . altered the truss wires to give an arch to the surfaces . . . Pass the beets, Katharine . . . Spliced the broken spars and ribs . . . we're ready to put the cloth back on . . ." *That's* interesting, not Rosie's dolls.

As for the grownups, I don't mess with them. Parents are strict, all of them. The Bishop is so stern, I think he's channeling the word of God. My parents are like him and I never disobey, don't even think of it. I never throw a temper tantrum; I say golly and dang in anger like everyone else and have to beg to go with the boys to Huffman's pasture for gliding, an afternoon of such harmless fun I'm always amazed at the effort it takes to get permission. But my parents usually give in, and because I'm a "good girl" and "no trouble," I'm allowed to go the next time—earned permission through good behavior. I'm trained and obedient.

The boys dress like accountants and wear starched white collars every day, bent over a drill in the shop or going headfirst off the rails at Kitty Hawk. There is no derring-do in Dayton, which seems right to me, and I think it is the best place in the world to live, which it probably is, what with Teddy Roosevelt charging around expanding the American Empire. It's early in our new century and the U.S. is in Cuba and even the Philippines, where the Senate finds us guilty of war crimes—big events and far-off. Yet right next door the boys are working on something really big and we don't realize it.

I too am at the edge of a big event and no one knows, certainly not me. I sit in our pear tree and watch the world go by.

Three

1903. DECEMBER 17.

My ninth birthday. Orville wires the Bishop from Kill Devil Hill at Kitty Hawk late in the afternoon: "Powered flight. Twelve seconds. Fifty-nine seconds by end of day."

From my perch in the pear tree I see the telegram arrive, know it's from the boys, and call over to Carrie.

"What does it say?"

"Not much." She's on the porch pulling her sweater close—it's cold. "Just the speed and distance this time"—and with a big smile—". . . they'll be back by Christmas." (Orville makes the turkey stuffing.)

I climb down and dart into our kitchen. I tell Mother the news and she's politely interested—Orville's stuffing is unparalleled.

It doesn't occur to me that Orville and Wil's flight should be treated like a big event. I don't wonder why reporters haven't already come inquiring: "How do you feel about the boys? Have they always wanted to do this?" "Well, yes. They work at it a good deal of the time."

The flight's under a minute. It's powered, the first in a world obsessed with the idea, but at fifty-nine seconds the *Dayton Journal* won't think it's worth an item. Won't mention it at all the next day.

We're a pretty evenhanded crowd in Dayton, tend away from drama.

I continue to run back and forth between our houses, getting information about the boys, checking on the baking of my birthday cake. The excitement mounts. It seems there can't be anything bigger or better or more dramatic that could happen and then Father walks in.

He hangs up his coat and turns to us.

"Teddy Roosevelt's building a canal," he says.

I go stock-still.

Four

"Going to finish the one the French started and they want me."

He's excited but doesn't show it. That's not his way, which is why I'm so captured by his news. He's always calm, but I can see in his eyes something is cooking.

Mother looks in from the kitchen. He takes a letter from his suit pocket and reads. "We are in the process of recruiting engineers and would like to interview you for a position." He looks up with a smile. "From the Panama Canal Commission." He has a square face, a balding head, and a relentlessly friendly demeanor.

Mother says nothing—not a good sign—but I'm used to her imposing presence, so it doesn't keep thoughts of Panama from swarming my mind, wondering where it is and what it's like and what all this means. Panama must be near the end of the world— it has to be wildly exciting.

The thought of a new life somewhere else suddenly trumps flying at Kitty Hawk or working in the boys' shop or even the modest celebration of my birthday. But I contain myself because demonstrations of emotion aren't allowed in our house. No squealing. No jumping.

Father knows how to navigate the moment. He slips the letter back into his suit pocket and turns to me. "How's my birthday girl?"

"Just fine. The boys flew."

"Did they, now?" (Small potatoes compared to Panama.) "Good for them."

This is when he'll settle with his paper into his overstuffed chair, turn on the radio, and wait for Mother's call to supper. But this time he doesn't do that. He sits, picks up the paper, and doesn't read a word. He doesn't once twirl the radio dial. Instead he smiles to himself, slips the Panama letter out of his pocket, and reads it again, which confirms my suspicions. With the second reading of the letter, I know it has to be a fantastic place.

I lean on the arm of his chair and bounce my legs off the floor.

"Where is Panama, Daddy?"

Five

AFTER 1903.

Mother rejects the idea of moving to Panama and Father begins the task of gentle persuasion. He brings up the subject discreetly over the months and the years, working on Mother but never overwhelming her—he knows how to do this. It's not unlike building a flying machine the Dayton way: dogged, with quiet perseverance.

Canal construction continues. So do letters from the Commission. I grow taller. The boys' flying machines grow bigger. Mother begins to give in, all this gradual.

She asks questions: schools, living accommodations, trips back home. Father gives her accurate information, especially about the colony called the Zone, a strip of land five miles on each side of the canal transformed into something totally American. No sudden culture shock for her to fear.

He wears her down like water on a stone.

Fifteen years old.

I'm a teenager. It's 1910. One day, for no reason I know, Panama comes up and Mother relents. "Only three years. It should be interesting," she says.

I can hardly believe my ears. After all this time and with only a few words she's caved. Father is elated but contains himself—the last years of construction are better than none. For me it's a rush of enormous excitement, a sea change in my life, which has become increasingly provincial and boring. I'm an adolescent and there are fires kindling in me that need a place to combust, which doesn't seem to be Dayton and by now I'm convinced is Panama—been nurturing that thought for years reading about the country, keeping up with canal stories. I'm instantly ready to go.

Our departure happens fast. Father leaves first, excited as a boy. Mother and I follow. I feign sadness at leaving school friends but I can't wait to hurtle toward the tropics. Mother is hoping the whole thing will pass quickly.

The Wrights promise to look after the house, which we carefully latch and lock. There are early-morning teary goodbyes from Katharine and Carrie and a stiff "good journey" from the Bishop. The boys, already at the shop, wished us well the evening before. I'm jumpy. The departure feels like it's taking forever.

We board a train to New York, then a boat to Panama, and that gets an item in the *Dayton Journal.*

"The William Haileys of number 9 Hawthorne Street have sailed for the Isthmus of Panama, where Mr. Hailey's expertise in railroad management will be added to the Canal Commission team."

We get a fourteen-point headline on page two.

Six

THE ADVANCE, THE PANAMA RAILROAD LINE'S VESSEL that plies between New York and the narrow strip of land called the Isthmus of Panama, is no grand ocean liner, but it's far from Dayton and puts me in a state of perpetual excitement.

We have a little cabin, good food, and a dose of seasickness— green with it for three days. We're hardly able to get to the cabin door when they bring us apples and crackers, and those don't stay down either. I'm miserable but I wouldn't go back for anything. If it's the price of traveling to adventure, I'll gladly pay it. Then suddenly the sickness is gone—soft-boiled eggs, a walk around the deck, and we have our sea legs.

For the first time we sit in deck chairs as we move down the Atlantic to the new world. Sun reflects so bright in our eyes, we have to cover them with scarves—no experience like this in Dayton. We're landlocked Buckeyes. This is my first sight of endless water, not to mention ocean liners—the stately ones we saw when we embarked in New York.

I feel cut loose but we're still with Americans. The passengers sitting near us are mostly women, all bound for the Canal Zone, returning from home leave. They talk among themselves and boast about their husbands' positions—sanitation officer, steamshovel engineer, materials expert—and it's soon evident that like us they're from all over the Midwest. Unlike us they're old hands at canal life.

We listen silently. Mother is socially shy, and though Father is a boss above all the positions the ladies are talking about, she isn't going to make that announcement. We look through our eyelashes to screen out the sun and the women continue to brag about their husbands' pay levels, where they live, and what kind of homes they've been given. In the middle of this shameless boasting Mother suddenly speaks up.

"My husband's working on the canal to prove his faith in Teddy Roosevelt and America."

The chatter stops. One of the women says, "That's very interesting."

It's a snub but Mother covers her eyes and doesn't notice. Gradually the chatter starts again but they keep it quiet and we're excluded. Mother's let it be known where she stands and that's enough. She turns her head away.

She actually disapproves of the way the Zone was acquired—American gunships in the harbor, Colombians told to leave, roughrider Teddy Roosevelt making sure Panama became autonomous so he can make his deal and build his canal. "Nothing democratic about that," Mother said when it was in the paper. "Who gave him those rights?"

I've recently read the Spanish Church thinks building the canal is blasphemous—if God wanted the oceans connected, he would have made them that way. Sitting on the sun-bloodied deck, I want to give her that piece of information to use against the snobby women. "You know, Mother . . ." She rolls her head toward me but I can't say it. "I can hardly wait to get there."

I didn't really want to say it, not on the high seas for the first time. She'd think the business about God objecting to the canal is absurd. We're Methodists, after all. We don't mix God and geography, and shoring her position against acquisition of the Isthmus with God as topographer is beneath her. Ludicrous. Good for her. Good for our family—sensible above all else.

They don't know I am resolved above all else to be less sensible.

Four days later we arrive in the Port of Colon, Panama.

Seven

PANAMA IS EVEN BETTER THAN I HOPED, thick with humidity, raucous noise, and heavy, sultry scents. I'm not in Dayton anymore.

The Chagres River cuts through the dense rainforest and disappears in ribbons of slick licorice blackness.

Big, leathery flowers surround us. Their exotic fragrance mixes with the smell of unfamiliar foods and oils.

Outrageous color is everywhere. Gorgeous, gaudy parrots swoop through treetops and flash yellow, blue, orange, and some wildly unnatural pink.

Dozens of languages come at us from faces that are black,

beige, yellow, or the Cuban Spaniards' white—it's all far more than I imagined.

Women are half naked, wrapped in brilliant colors, wearing turbans. They carry fruit and babies and walk with an undulating indifference I've never seen before. I want that, that cool half-weary walk so unlike anybody in Dayton, a state of mind in a lazy gait. Amazing.

And running through all this a few yards from the footpath is the canal itself. The center of everything. Not a ditch. Not even a big ditch. It's the largest man-made canyon on planet Earth and they call it the Cut. Filled with laborers and machinery as far as the eye can see, this teeming mix of metal, flesh, and boulder spreads gaping beside us as Mother and I ride along wide-eyed in the gleaming Canal Commission passenger train taking us to Culebra, fifty miles on the other side of the Isthmus. Panama runs east–west. The canal and the Zone and the Commission railroad run north–south. I picture it as we ride, my map study paying off.

The Zoner ladies from the ship are seated nearby and pay little attention to us or to the new world outside; it's not new to them. But we're first-timers and we're dazzled. The blinding sun, the sounds, and smells boggle us into silence.

In Culebra, Father is waiting, smiling to see us. He's so excited, he hugs us twice each. He keeps saying, "My best girls," then wipes his forehead and replaces his hat. It's not a fedora. It's a heat-worthy woven hat with a wide brim, the kind worn by the bosses, the Americans in charge. Father's a canal boss and stands out in the crowd. I puff a little with pride.

"Be careful, now," he says and helps us into a horse-drawn

wagon. There's a Canal Commission emblem on the side and a canvas canopy on wobbly poles protecting us from the sun.

"Comfortable?" he asks.

"Pretty hot," Mother says.

"You'll get used to it."

I'm suffocating.

Eight

THE DRIVER CLUCKS TO HIS NAG. We move off and Father starts talking. I've never heard anything like it, not from my reserved father. He's usually quiet and thoughtful, speaking when he's spoken to. But now, this unbridled enthusiasm that Midwesterners take pains to avoid, because it's too revealing of emotion and too fast, pours out of him. He speaks with no restraint and his enthusiasm is simply harmless bubbling energy. It's genuine. Mother knows that, although I can see it puts her off a little.

He recites details of canal construction and of his work. Mother responds with "How is that, again?" and "Good heavens." On he goes, a hyped rattle that interests me just because it's from Father and so unlike him.

"It's organized. Whole operation runs like clockwork, department for everything—supplies, personnel, living quarters, buildings, architecture"—Mother smiles at his rush of words—"machinery, of course, and maps, topographical and substrata— we use those every day . . . and there's a printing and climatic-conditions department, and river hydraulics because we're so close to the Chagres, and the communications department—we'd be lost without them . . ." I've never heard him say this many words at one time. ". . . all set up before I got here, of course—engineers worked it out—" And he's about to go on but . . . "Ah, look. Now you can see it."

The Cut in full view below us.

It seems we've landed on another planet.

Half a mile across at the top, thousands of laborers on the floor looking like insects. Trains stacked up the side moving back and forth, carrying off dirt and rock. All of it, men and machines, minuscule in the distance against the vast excavation.

"Yours?" Mother asks. "The trains?"

"Yep. And on the far side, see the trackshifter?" A steel pterodactyl is dozing there. "Darnedest thing," he says. "Picks up the rails every evening and moves them like toys. Workers find out where to show up in the roundhouse each morning." He shakes his head in wonder. And he's not done yet. He points in another direction.

"See those steam shovels? They're ninety-five tons each. Outfit called Bucyrus makes them for us. Three times the size of anything you'll ever see in Dayton—anywhere else, for that matter. Two men on each shovel—one controls the crane and picks up dirt, the other's got his hands and feet on levers to control the rest of the machine. They're like bronco riders, those fellas." Then, with genuine respect, "Strong, thick-skinned boys—they're in that blasting and heat six days a week. It's hard work and dangerous."

It looks like he's finished for a while and he gazes at the operation satisfied.

Mother clears her throat. She sits ramrod straight as though in our quiet Dayton home. "Well, it certainly is going to be one of the wonders of the world," she says. Father grins.

I finally pipe in. "Where does the dirt go?"

"Gatun Dam in the Chagres. Whole towns being built on that landfill."

Nine

As wonderful as everything is (I've seen nothing like the Cut ever in my life), I'm still watching for something really exotic, not sure yet what that would be. I badly want my life to change. So I can't help being disappointed when we arrive at our new-world house that looks very much like the old-world house in Dayton—typical Midwestern clapboard with a long screened porch. Maybe I was expecting a thatched roof, I don't know.

Mother isn't disappointed—it's what Father promised. "Will you look at that," she says, a big smile at the familiar structure.

Inside it's the same layout as our house in Dayton (these Canal Commission builders knew how to replicate the heartland). Nice living room, kitchen with laundry, and dining room on the first floor. Two bedrooms and bath above. Plenty of closet space. Rockers on the porch. "So you can watch the sunset," Father says. Then he says to the black men who've unloaded our cases, *"Gracias. Ustedes pueden vayar."*

Now, that's something different. Spanish from Father—simple, proper, but effective, and the men leave, just as he told them to.

Father begins pushing the sofa nearer a window according to

Mother's orders and I see that furniture arranging could go on for a while. I go upstairs.

My room looks across the Cut and it's better than the one in Dayton, if only because it's empty. It's a grown-up room—plain, no pictures on the wall, none of my drawings trying to be young Michelangelo with sepia pencil crosshatching. Just clean, bare walls and a big window.

I've brought some light clothing and a few notebooks and that's it, no décor. I'm going to leave it simple. Adult and not Dayton.

In the evening when we are "put away" and "hung up," Mother discovers ants threading across the kitchen floor. She sweeps them out. Father plasters puttylike goo around the door and windows. I scrub up.

Mother cooks us a fine little meal from the goods Father has laid in and all's well.

When we go upstairs and fall into bed, I wonder if my parents will make love after being apart so long, but the thought is only a streak through my teen brain already packed with uneasy excitement. I keep wondering if this is it, the place I've conjured for years. Does it match my fantasy?

I lie in bed and study the shadows on my ceiling, leafy and stretched oblong, not so different from the ones in Dayton. I try to work out what I feel about this new place, think I'll never fall asleep. Then the scent of Mother's Dayton soap in the sheets blurs me and I'm anesthetized into deep, dark Panama night.

The fantasy is out there. I'll find it.

Ten

AND I DO. But not right away. It gets worse before it gets better. I continue to be cranky with the heat and look to Mother for sympathy, but I get none. She's doing fine and that too irritates me.

Her cake falls from the daily blasting that shakes the house and the oven but it doesn't bother her. She serves "flat cake" with thick dollops of whipped cream. It's delicious. So is everything else she makes. Panama's fruit and vegetables are abundant and fresh and cause some inner chef to bloom in her, producing wonderful platters unlike any she ever concocted in Dayton. As for her new house, it's better than the one she left behind. So all in all, the place she dreaded is not dreadful in any way. She's content.

But not me.

After a week I realize with a fair amount of horror that the Zone is really just like Dayton. It's meant to be. And not just the houses. Coming to us in weekly boatloads are favorite American foods, books, magazines, clothing, and hardware, as though we were on Main Street U.S.A. All around us are the familiar men's clubs—Kiwanis, Elks, Masons—and women's groups and all in English—there's not even a foreign language. It's devastating. All the hope and expectation built up in me is drained away. Even hopes that school would be different with kids from other lands speaking different languages are crushed. (What was I thinking?) It's just like Dayton—American kids from Zoner families. No workers' kids at all, and they're the ones I want to know.

I go to school by train, the only thing that's entirely new. Balboa High is in Cristobal, forty miles on the other side of the Isthmus. But the building is wood clapboard like all the others—square and functional, with an occasional breeze through screened windows—very Midwestern.

The students are bored, uninteresting adolescents full of pranks and pimples. Nothing new there.

"Where are you from?" says one.

"Dayton," I say. "You?"

"Indianapolis."

"You're good at art," I say. "I saw your drawings. I'd really like to see what else you've d—"

"See that boy over there? I think he likes me."

"Where?" This Hoosier girl points him out.

Nothing's different. Boy-crazy girls and friendship by way of collusion. Nobody remotely like the Wrights. Certainly nobody inventing anything.

A few weeks after arrival I go sullen.

The train ride is always social hour, so there I continue to make an effort. I engage in friendly gab as best I can. Of course, I disguise what I think of these morons, while outside the train are indigenous Panamanians and workers from everywhere in the world, literally, with lives and stories I've never heard. *I WANT TO MEET THEM.*

I lower the train window and hang out. Hot wind whips my hair. Those women with children and baskets on their heads and the workers in the Cut aren't really so distant, but I might as well be watching from the moon. I can't reach them. I'm sequestered in the American Zone.

Twice a day on the train I go through this mental anguish, looking at the exotic world I want to know, and I wind tighter with resentment each trip. It's not good.

Provincial weeks turn into provincial months. I go from sulky to resentful. I'm morose. On a good day I brood, but Mother's narrow-eyed look keeps me in line so I don't act on my feelings or talk about them, which makes them worse.

I start a diary where I spill my discontent.

I begin to go whole days without speaking.

I overhear Mother say to Father: "She's growing up."

Yeah.

ALONG COMES HARRY
Eleven

AT LAST.

Harry's not the love of my life. He's more the brother I never had, better than the boys, more suitable to my near-adult self, and he'll get me to whatever it is I want—I know it the moment I meet him. He's the connection.

It happens like this.

I'm staring at our living-room rug one evening. It's a dark green leaf design. I'm thinking it's as close as I'll ever get to the rainforest, which at that point was probably true. That makes me crazy. Everything does. The hellish humidity, my boring life, everything. I'm groggy and sticky. I'm sixteen. I'm pondering two more years of this deathtrap. I feel so bad, I can't read the book beside me. Thank God I've perfected not showing my crankiness.

"How's everything?" Father says. (He noticed?) He lets the top half of his paper droop. He peers at me. "Are you doing okay, sport?"

(Sport is my kid moniker. What's going on?)

"I'm okay," I say.

"Just okay?"

"Well . . . I'm kind of unhappy. I don't know."

This is his time to read the paper, wait for supper, like in Dayton. But he seems to want to know what's going on with me and I'm baffled. It's new.

"I guess I miss the boys," I say.

"Why, sure you do. I do too. New place like this, you're going to miss your friends." (We've been here a year.) "Nobody you like at school?"

The first query about my life and adjusting. What a corseted family we are.

"No, not really," I say. "Not interesting ones that I like. But that's probably just me being picky." There's a smoky smell— some clearing is going on down the hill, the usual brush burning.

"Well, I wouldn't say that. You're not picky." He puts down the paper, gives me his full attention. All the way to Panama to break the Victorian ice in our family.

I don't really think I'm picky either, but we both know I can't voice a complaint because Mother won't allow it. He knows how difficult that is and he knows how it feels living in such a strained atmosphere.

"Well now, we can't have that. Everybody needs friends."

I smile and move over to the ottoman in front of his chair.

"I complain to my diary."

"You do?"

"Write in it every day. How the men are in the Cut working all day and the women just gossip and the girls at school are too old to play dolls so they talk about romance. That's all they do. They've never heard of the Wrights' machine and they wouldn't care about it if they did . . ."

"Oh, for heaven's sake."

"It's true. The girls whisper about the boys and who they like or don't like and it's stupid. I miss Orville and Wil."

"Well, it's not easy to find people like them, but there are interesting people here."

"I haven't met one."

"Then we'd better take care of that. Come with me to the Canal Club on Saturday for lunch. I'll introduce you to an interesting fella."

This is so out of character, I don't know what to say. I grin. "Thanks, Pop. Who's the interesting person?"

"Harry."

"American?"

He nods. "You'll like him. Works for the Zone police. Closest thing you'll find to the boys. Smart, too. A high-quality fella, has horse sense." This is the single-most prized quality in our family.

I'm smiling, loving this. He's smiling, too. He raises his paper and I go back to my spot on the couch.

Did that really happen?

I speculate about this fellow—who he is, what he's all about. I know nothing, of course, except that he's passed Father's muster, which is considerable. In all of this there is a glimmer of hope.

"What's his name again?"

"Harry."

I sit back and grin.

The smoky smell reminds me of fall in Dayton when people burn their leaves.

WHO ARE YOU, HARRY?

Twelve

THE CANAL CLUB, SATURDAY, layers of white tablecloths, gauzy white curtains in the breeze, American faces except for servers.

This better be good. My nerves have been clutched for three days in anticipation—my imagination running riot, a measure of how desperate I am.

Father nods to several Commission bigwigs when we enter and we're led to a prominent table in the front of the room near a window. I realize for the first time how respected Father is, how well positioned in the Commission hierarchy. I like it. And I'm nervous.

A waiter approaches—very tall, very black, with a mellow Caribbean accent. "Good afternoon."

He places menus in our hands and leaves us to study them.

"The fish comes from the bay outside the window," Father says. "It's fresh."

Nice to know. There are chicken plates and salads and cold cuts, a nice selection. We sit silently going over the various dishes, me nervous, and then a voice says, "Hello."

I look up.

Harry. It has to be. A big, wide smile—nothing inscrutable there.

"I'm sorry I'm late. Police nonsense . . . paperwork . . ." He shakes Father's hand and nods to me.

"You're not late," says Father and introduces us.

Harry shakes my hand and looks me in the eye, whole sectors of me coming to attention that have been asleep for years, some for a lifetime.

Chairs scrape the floor and we settle in.

I can't take my eyes off him. He's of medium height, with clear blue eyes and perfect white teeth. He wears khaki police shorts and shirt, high boots, and the standard-issue wide-brimmed police hat, which he sticks under his chair. He's younger than the Wrights. Midtwenties, I estimate.

"Sure be glad when the rain starts," he says.

Father agrees and they make canal small talk. I want badly to join in but can't think of a thing to say, so I listen like a good girl.

Harry mentions he came down from Costa Rica, not from the States, and was "somewhere else in Central America before that."

He's an adventurer. This is getting better and better.

We order: fruit and some kind of chicken for all of us.

I ask him how he got his job. "Was it difficult?"

"Not really. I speak Spanish and a couple of other languages. That helped."

"They just signed you up?"

"Not exactly. I thought they'd want diggers—didn't know they don't use whites for that. But I filled out forms anyway and said a few words in Spanish and they hired me on the spot. It's the languages they wanted."

"Amazing."

"They made me census taker."

"First census taker I ever met," I say. I get a laugh with that. It feels good and I push the hair off my neck.

"Enumerator is what they call me."

"What do you do?"

"I go through the entire population of workers one by one. I'm doing a human accounting of this great dirt-shoveling congress," he says and laughs.

It makes me smile. This is a turn of words no common Midwesterner would use. I'm struck. It's not love—I don't have a crush on Harry. I'm knocked out by what he is because it's what I want to be and it's sitting beside me in the flesh, talking and laughing. It's unassuming and leading the footloose life I want so badly.

"So you meet all the workers?" I say.

He nods. "Much more interesting than digging," and he goes on, seeing our interest. He talks about the people, the work they do, what their world is like, and about himself.

"Found out I could go almost anywhere steerage and it's cheap—free if I do a little work on board. I can go where I want if I'm willing to work, and I am." That big grin. He's a vagabond.

We eat, talk, get into a short conversation about our families back in the States, and Father makes the offhand remark that Mother's people are from Kentucky.

Harry grins. "My grandfather was a telegrapher for the L.H. & St.L. Railroad in Irvington."

Father's surprised. "Well, for heaven's sake," he says. "That little town's just down the road from my wife's folks."

With that Harry becomes the rare man Father can trust with his firstborn or his life savings. It's not wandering freedom that gets Father—that's what gets me. It's Harry's roots—where a man comes from—that Father puts his stock in.

"Irvington man, eh?"

"Grandfather was."

A lull. Our plates are cleared by the quiet black man. I seize the moment.

"I'd sure like to come along when you enumerate."

Harry doesn't hesitate. "That's no problem, but it's almost always at night—only time the workers can talk."

"Can I go, Father?"

Harry: "There's a lot of climbing through brush to get to the labor camps . . ."

Me: "Great, great." Father doesn't know what to do. "I'll write about it for school. Please, Daddy, can I go?" I haven't called him Daddy in a decade.

Hesitation. Small dishes of pineapple sherbet are placed before us.

"I'll have to speak to your mother."

Thirteen

MOTHER COULD STOP ALL OF THIS IF SHE DECIDES TO. Harry's my ticket to freedom, but Mother's not keen on adventure, not in a jungle, not at night with someone she doesn't know.

A Harry/Mother meeting is arranged. It goes well, of course. What's not to like about Harry? His clean-cut looks, his manner, his background? He's from Kentucky and a sometime teacher— Mother taught until she married. He scores big with her on every point and yet, when he's gone . . .

"It's just not proper for a man in his midtwenties to be out with a girl of sixteen in the middle of the night." Does she think all men are predatory animals except for Father? "It's a temptation and it doesn't look right."

"He wouldn't lay a hand on her."

"It's not right."

Father hangs in, defends Harry, and because Mother trusts Father's judgment and really does like Harry, she doesn't say no, just that she wants to think more about it.

I go up to my room, jittery. I can't sit still. I need an answer. I need it to be yes. I need to throw something, hit something, make noise, break things, do something wild and out of control, but I don't. I'm trained not to. I look in the mirror. My face is breaking out.

Downstairs an hour later, when she gives permission for me to go, I literally jump for joy, give her a hug, and bound back up the steps two at a time.

In my room I dance a jig, quietly. Soundlessly leap on my bed and pump my legs in place, my arms in the air, eyes squinting. I throw back my head in a silent howl of joy. This is how victory sounds in our house. My diary gets the noisy announcement: *Guess what I'm going to do?!!! Harry's going to save me! He's going to make things all right!*

Freedom, Sort Of

Fourteen

It's eight o'clock in the evening on the appointed Thursday. I'm in fevered anticipation, wearing jodhpurs and high-top shoes, ready to go out with Harry, feeling great. This is what I want, what I thought I'd get all those years of waiting and thinking about Panama. A great adventure in the dead of night. After supper, anyway.

The jodhpurs are what I wore when I went to Huffman's pasture with the boys—practical but hot. Loose pants or khaki shorts like Harry's would be cooler but Mother won't hear of it. "Scratches and insects and snakes," she says. I have to cover my legs, wear lace-up leather footgear. I'm too happy to complain.

Harry has told me that in the field he carries a white canvas bag with his field notebook, red cards to tag the canvassed buildings, and a certificate to show he's the official census taker. Not many workers can read, but the sight of him in police uniform with the certificates makes him look official. That's what matters. All this is more than I could have hoped for and better than helping Wil and Orville. Harry is my new Wright brother, a more worldly one.

Mother and Father see us off, standing at the top of the stairs. "Be careful."

From down on the track we give them a wave and start walking fast along the rails in the moonlight. This is the road to everywhere, used by everyone, on foot or by train.

"Stay close," Harry says.

He walks in front. We hardly exchange a word, only stride along in the sultry night. We pass a few individuals who nod or greet us in Spanish. "... *buena* ..."

Looming ahead, the abandoned French locomotives appear ghostlike, rusted, the remains of their fiasco a decade earlier. Beautiful old machines, vines growing into them. They look like sunken vessels. I slow briefly to sketch and Harry calls back: "Come on, stay close."

We hustle along for nearly half an hour. It's pitch-black. The heat is oppressive but for the first time I don't care.

Finally we come to Cunette, the laborers' camp. Barracks and dim lights.

"Stay behind me," Harry says. We approach the first barrack.

He moves the canvas flap aside and steps in.

Fifteen

QUARTERS FOR THE COMMON LABORERS, ALL OF THEM BLACK. It's little more than a tent with a wooden floor. I can't see anything for a few minutes—Harry's figure in the door blocks my view but I hear his voice.

"Buenas noches . . ."

In fluent Spanish he tells them who he is, what he's doing. I've had lots of Spanish and know it well, but I can't speak like Harry. No American accent at all. It rolls out of him fast and easy like a mother tongue. I see why he was hired on the spot.

There isn't a sound from the men inside—their animated talk has stopped. Harry holds his questionnaire clipped to a board and starts with the closest worker.

"Name?"

"David Providence." The man speaks English—he's clearly from the islands.

"Metal number?"

He recites his number. The others are mute.

I want to see all this and I move closer. I peer in: two rows of double-sided three-story bunks—strips of canvas on gas pipes that can be hung up like folded swinging shelves when they aren't in use. At two tables, eighteen or so Negroes are in undershirts and trousers—their card game suspended, anxiety in their eyes, looking at two white faces usually seen only when there has been a crime. Harry isn't threatening. He's respectful, but they still look uneasy. They sit barely moving.

Harry finishes with David Providence and starts with a new worker.

"What's your name?"

"Levi McCarthy."

"Metal-check number?" McCarthy recites his number. "Haven't I seen you in the Canal Club, McCarthy?"

"I am a waiter."

I take a closer look. There is our waiter from the day I met Harry. He lives here in Cunette.

I'm shocked. I don't know how I pictured him. Going home, maybe, to a nice little house or apartment somewhere, the way a waiter might in Dayton, but not like this.

He speaks with dignity, answers Harry's questions. But it looks all wrong. In the club he is tall and quiet, seems perfectly correct. But here, among the hanging canvas cots in a laborers' barrack, he seems displaced. In his uniform he's impressive—could pass for the leader of an African nation. Here, in an undershirt and loose trousers, his skin shining with sweat, he's diminished, unimportant, his footprint on planet Earth a few square feet of cot and belongings.

Harry moves to the next man. I don't take my eyes off McCarthy.

Harry's voice: "Your name?" The man doesn't understand.

"Cummun t'appelle?" Harry switches to Cajun. It works. *"Cajevous?"* His age, the kind of work he does, how long he's been there—Harry gets it all with his easy authority.

I don't say a word. I stand behind him trying to be invisible, watching McCarthy and the others. From time to time the eyes of laborers flick toward me. *Who is she? Why is she with Harry? His woman? His daughter? His tightlipped assistant?*

Mostly they watch Harry going from man to man. They're all from different locales, speak various languages. Some don't understand the simplest queries, but Harry is efficient. He finds some hybrid of dialects that works and every man responds.

"Beresford Plantaganet." (No need to ask if he's a British subject.)

"'Rasmus Iggleston." (From Montserrat.)

"Smith." (From St. Vincent.) "Married, but my wife and child haven't arrived yet—a baby born last week." Harry moves his pencil to a new spot on the form.

"Will they be living with you?"

"Yes, in the married quarters."

"What's the name of the child?"

"He was just baptized . . ." Smith has to refer to an entry in the Bible by his cot. "Hazarmaneth Cumberbath Smith."

Not a flinch from Harry. The impressive name goes on his record. He gives the man a nod and moves on.

I look again at our waiter, McCarthy. He's watching all this silently with the others.

Sixteen

So my new Panama life begins, what I wanted all along. Very nearly.

Eyes wide open I see men from Costa Rica, Guatemalteco, Venezuela, Trinidad. From barrack to barrack that night for hours, I see and hear more different kinds of humanity than I've ever seen or read about in my life.

In the early hours of morning we're at the last place, a small cabin. We wake five Punjabis. They're drowsy, can't make out what Harry is all about. He says three words in their language and they spring to life. They can't believe their ears. We're invited in, lights go on, we're offered tea. They smile and talk, but Harry keeps it respectful and businesslike—census work only, not a social call. He completes their forms, and they stand at the door watching with wide grins as Harry tacks a red completion tag on the outside of the cabin. The whole thing has taken no more than a quarter of an hour.

"They're going to think they dreamed the visit from a white man who spoke their language in the middle of the night," he says.

"No, they won't."

"I mispronounced the Punjabi."

"Don't think they noticed."

We hurry along the track toward my house. I can't get the workers out of my mind. "Why aren't there any American blacks?"

"Canal Commission doesn't want them. They only want men from the islands and Europe and the Orient. Skilled whites from the States only, no blacks."

"Why not?"

"They call them 'corrupting States niggers.'" He glances at me. Sees I'm shocked. "You never heard anything like that in Dayton, did you?"

"No."

"American blacks might expect too much, being free now," he says. "Labor has to be cheap, keep the cost down. Desperate men work for nearly nothing—for food if you give them a little." We're walking so fast that I'm out of breath, and my real education has begun, the one about the world. Maybe that's what took my breath away. He talks some more about the poor black workers, then at my back door I say: "I want to come again. Can I? Please?"

He smiles at my enthusiasm. "Sure, just let me know." He says goodbye and starts back down the stairs.

He likes me, I can tell—likes my questions. I'm not a pest and I'm earnest. And he won't mind my company from time to time.

Mother is in her robe in the kitchen. "It was wonderful," I say. "Did you wait up?"

"No. I heard your voices." That's it. She's satisfied—I'm safely home. "Take a shower and jump in bed." This is not the time to negotiate more outings.

I go up the steps two at a time. The 4:30 whistle sounds for the laborers—another hellish day for them in the Cut. More than ever I wonder how they do it.

Seventeen

SCHOOL. I make an announcement to Mrs. Ewing: "I've been to the workers' camps with the enumerator." She looks at me a little shocked. "Cunette and some others. I'm doing an extra-credit paper on it."

"How in the world . . . ?"

"My parents allowed it. I want to go again, a lot more times." She's perplexed. Her sullen but dutiful student has come to life. "I've only seen a little, so I need to go again and learn more."

"How did you arrange it?"

I tell her about Harry—meeting him through Father, what he's doing. She's impressed and I pop the question.

"Would you encourage Mother to allow me to go a few more

times? Teacher to teacher—you know, send a note?" She hesitates. "It's good research training and I'm going to need that in college . . ."

"Yes, you certainly will . . ."

I skid into the kitchen and lay the note on the counter next to Mother, who's kneading dough. I know the letter's contents.

- A unique opportunity.
- The loss of sleep well worth what she'll learn.
- Safe with the enumerator, a respected member of the police force working directly with the quartermaster's office.

(Mrs. Ewing's husband works there—she knows all about Harry. A huge bonus.)

- Please allow the visits with Harry to continue. The class will benefit, et cetera, et cetera. (Straightforward, clear, persuasive.)

Mother looks up at me. "How often do you want to go?"

"Twice a week."

"You'll be half asleep in school the next day."

"I'll nap on the train."

She thinks it over. Rolls out the dough.

"A pie?" I ask. She doesn't hear me. I see her thinking hard. Then:

"We'll try it. But only once a week."

Eighteen

ONCE A WEEK AND NOW THERE'S MOMENTUM.

Every week I go with Harry barrack to barrack, and he tells me what he's learned firsthand in his years of wandering—my education continues. He talks about how hard it is for the poor. How the destitute outnumber the rich. How "someday they'll rise to justice, but not in my lifetime, or in my children's, even. The rich are too strong. They have all the advantages." I've never heard anybody talk like this. It's a wild world I'm learning about, and it's not just in books.

". . . peasants in every country," Harry says, "and their back-breaking labor is what makes the aristocracy rich, even in America." This grinds inside him. He'll go on and on about it if I encourage him, which I always do. I need to hear it and he must need to talk about it, because he has plenty to say.

"I've seen cruelties you wouldn't believe. Thousands of workers doing soul-crushing work to blast a road through a mountain, or a tunnel through some elevation"—flings his arm toward the Cut—"or a canal through igneous rock that's not meant to be split by anything but continental drift, and all so commerce can make the privileged richer." We walk toward my house, the end of another night's work. "Americans are reaping the profit of cheap labor all over the world—I've seen it." He shakes his head. This eats at him the way being sequestered from the people ate at me.

I want to say something, put in my two cents, but I don't. I'm a student. A provincial girl from Dayton, Ohio, and I listen. On nights like this I want to be just like Harry; gender has nothing to do with it.

At the end of the long evenings, Mother meets me in the kitchen. She shakes her head and says nothing. I'm sweaty, unladylike. It disturbs her. The furrow between her eyes deepens— this is no way for a young lady to grow up. She hopes I'll lose interest but I don't.

And then, though I couldn't ask for anything more, more finds me.

Harry and Ruby

Nineteen

It begins with Mrs. McManus.

Harry becomes a regular at our house for dinner, an avuncular presence. It's clear he sees me as a student, a good-natured niece. He's family. And we learn more about him, some rather unexpected news. He tells us he's seeing Mrs. McManus from Nebraska.

"She was widowed last year, wasn't she?" says Mother.

"A locomotive went wild." Harry holds a forkful of green beans in midair. "He was crushed between two flatcars."

Father looks up, knows all about this incident.

"They tried to keep her from seeing the body but she insisted. That's why she took it so hard, I think, seeing her husband that way." He chews the bite of beans, studies his plate.

Mother leans forward. "And she had some kind of . . . breakdown, was it?" Even Mother can't resist these further details.

"I wouldn't call it a breakdown." Those are neurotic-sounding words to Midwestern ears, even to vagabond Harry's. The scent of

Mother's just-baked lemon pie hangs in the air. Harry ponders a moment longer, then says, "She was grieving is all, no breakdown. I'm not sure how much she's over it. She feels things . . . deeply."

"Of course."

He shakes his head, swirls a neat chunk of pork in the sauce. "We are . . ." He wants to go on but hesitates, then says, "I find her a very bright woman. We have people in common, friends of mine that know her people." Another swirl in the sauce. "I've been calling on her. It's a comfort for her to have a friend." The chunk of pork goes into his mouth and he chews, thoughtful.

So Harry's got a quiet love affair. Secretive. Revealed to us in confidence.

"Of course," says Mother.

I have goose bumps on my arms.

A few days later I find out her full name standing in line at the commissary. The cashier calls her Ruby and she pays keeping her eyes down. Ruby McManus, about thirty, is extremely pretty, and she doesn't look at me or anyone else directly. It gives her a mysterious appearance, something that's not at all Midwestern. I can see why that attracts Harry. Mystery is seductive. To some of us, anyway. Good for Harry. His relationship with the widow McManus is about to work in my favor.

I hear Mother talking to Father that evening in their room: ". . . more comfortable seeing her go out at night with Harry knowing he has a female companion." I realize I'll be going with

Harry more often, which is just what I've wanted, and I feel a bump of elation, then, suddenly, anxiety, which I can't figure out. It's strange. It's not about Harry—being with Harry more often can only be good. The anxiety is about me. I sense something.

The planets are aligned. Everything is in place. Something is coming and I'm uneasy about it. That's what it is. Look, I don't believe in the dreamy premonitions people talk about—my feet are planted squarely on the ground—but something is imminent. I can feel it and it keeps me awake. I don't eat well and I'm easily distracted.

Something is close, I write in my diary. *Don't know what it could be.*

Twenty

I BEGIN GOING WITH HARRY TWICE A WEEK, and on a dark, moonless night of the second week, this imminent thing happens. I don't see it coming at all. It is an evening like many others with Harry.

"We'll be going to worker cabins this time," he says, and off we go in a different direction, across a field of stubble, through some trees, along the Cut. We come to a long line of small structures, the cabins housing laborers by their country of origin. Harry goes to work.

He knocks at the doors, calls out greetings in Spanish. The responses come in various tongues—Chinese, Greek, Danish,

Portuguese, in the first hour alone. Harry impresses me all over again with his uncanny ear. He has an amazing gift for language.

Chinese almost stumps him, but with hand signs and a few words in Mandarin, he gets his questions answered.

"I'll go there one day," he says as he tacks the red tag on the Chinese cabin.

"It's so far."

"Steerage."

"Ah, right." And he'll learn the language, too, I have no doubt.

We hike to a dozen cabins with workers jammed into junk-jumbled rooms, very different from the barracks. Fewer men, smaller spaces. These are wretched shacks, not cabins. But none of this figures in my premonition—not so far, anyway.

I busy myself taking notes: the look of the place, the total lack of hygiene, everything filthy and broken. And the whole camp reeks. Cans and papers are thrown out doors. Boxes litter the space between structures. Bits of rag hang off sagging rails. Maybe shirts or what's left of them out to dry—a hopeless process in a sultry jungle.

All this is material for essays, observations on the canal's working class larded with Harry's fire about the laborers' burden. Mrs. Ewing will love it. Still, I feel the uncertainty. It's not fear. It's an unsettledness—is that a word?

We move on, saying very little to each other. My notes keep me occupied.

We come to a cabin that's not like the others. There is no

debris outside, not a scrap of paper or a tin can. It's so clean, it seems uninhabited. This is it. The totally unpredicted. The unpredictable, imminent thing.

Here's where my life is about to change.

Twenty-one

"MAYBE NO ONE'S LIVING HERE," HARRY SAYS.

I look closely. "But there's a light."

A glow comes from the window. We go to the screened door and knock. In well-articulated Castilian, a voice tells us to enter.

There must be some mistake. No worker talks like that.

We step into a freshly scrubbed, well-ordered cabin with clean cots, a small table, and a hammock. A Spaniard is sitting alone reading, one foot propped on the only other chair.

He looks at us, undisturbed and calm, no trace of alarm. He wears newly washed work clothes. He's holding a thick book with worn pages. This cabin is so orderly and clean, it could be a vacation hideaway in the Adirondacks, but a worker sits there, a man Harry's age. I can't take my eyes off him.

"You live here alone?" Harry says in smooth Castilian.

"No. My roommate is next door—a card game."

Harry nods.

I've never heard elegant Castilian before. They sound like two diplomats, not worker and census taker.

Harry takes a seat on an empty cot and I sit beside him. I look around the room, intimidated. On the wall is an unpainted shelf made of dynamite boxes. It's filled with books, and there are more books on the table.

Harry begins to reel off questions.

"Name?"

"Federico Malero."

"Metal-check number?"

He answers without moving, book in hand. I'm glued to his elegant speech and his impressive calm.

He just doesn't move, doesn't even close the book. His answers are quick and precise. Harry finally comes to the last question and I'm still transfixed.

"Can you read?"

Harry reads off the question as he does all the others—looking at the form, pencil poised. Malero answers with a faint smile and a slightly condescending tone.

"A little," he says in perfect British-educated English.

Harry's head jerks up. The Spaniard nods toward the shelf.

"My library."

An intrigued smile comes over Harry's face. He gets up, goes to the shelf, and studies the titles: Barcelona paper editions of Hegel, Fichte, Spencer, Huxley, and others, all of them dog-eared from reading.

"Mine and my roommate's," says Malero.

Harry turns to him and frowns, confused. "You're a foreman and living here?"

"Pico y pala."

"Pick and shovel? Dirt gang, and you read those?" Harry is baffled. So am I, with my other loopy feelings.

"It doesn't matter," Malero says.

He's still unperturbed and offers no explanation. His smile is distant, mysterious. Dark, wavy hair, fair complexion but tanned from work in the sun. Long fingers, one slipped behind a page ready to turn it. He's handsome, self-assured, impeccable, and a pick-and-shovel worker in the Cut. It's impossible.

Since we came in, he's only raised his head. We haven't troubled him—we certainly haven't scared him.

"Well then . . ." Harry says.

He wants a conversation with this Malero, I see it. This educated European working in the Cut—just the kind of fellow Harry would like to know, talk politics with, be personal with. But disciplined Harry does as he's hired to do. He makes out a red completion tag for the side of the cabin.

Federico glances at me for the first time. I'm suddenly self-conscious and close my mouth, flick my eyes around, heart thumping.

"Where's your roommate, again?" Harry says, tag finished.

"Next cabin playing cards."

"That's right. I'll catch him there."

Hesitation. Harry wants badly to talk. But he doesn't. He says, "All right then," and reaches out to shake Malero's hand, something he never does with other laborers.

Still Federico does not get up or move, only shakes Harry's hand and says goodbye. He will not be disturbed.

Federico goes back to his book and Harry and I go to the door.

I glance back at Federico, who raises his eyes to me. I turn away in confusion and go out.

I'm shaken.

Twenty-two

"MAYBE I SHOULD HAVE JOINED THE PICK-AND-SHOVEL GANG," Harry says, tacking the red tag on Federico's cabin. "I may have missed something. Look who's working there. Pick and shovel with a mind like that?"

"You could ask him about it." I'm rattled, my heart booming, but I'm ready to walk back in.

"No, no socializing. Maybe it's more money than he can earn in Spain."

"Maybe."

"Or he's running away from something . . ."

"Yeah."

Harry goes on guessing. I'm not hearing. Federico fills my mind—no space for anything else. His face and hands, the way he sits, how comfortable he is with himself, in some other world, one I want to know.

Gradually Harry's voice comes back. ". . . more educated than his bosses and swinging pick and shovel. Bet the steam shovelers condescend to him, call him 'spig,' and he's European and better read than any of them . . ." He mutters on. Of course, he's right.

No doubt the shovelers patronize Federico the way they do all the diggers, treat him like an animal because he's beneath them. Call him "spig" because all the immigrants say "spigadaEnglish." Degrading.

But Malero is no pig-English laborer. He's got a story—it's

obvious. And more than that, he's beautiful. And that is what I'm visualizing: Federico sitting at his desk with a book, perfect, like a photograph. In my brain his image comes into focus with the one that's been floating there for years—a spiky urging in me since Father first spoke the word Panama. A smoky, intuited vagueness that formed slowly and became a shape that represents all I don't know. Outside the cabin I realize Federico Malero is that shape. At least, I think he is.

I'm fully awake for the first time. Fully conscious, the fog blown away. Everything is sharp.

Calm, intelligent Federico, a few yards away, is now that image, my center of gravity. I no longer feel I have to get somewhere else or escape. I'm present, in the moment. In the middle of the worst stubble and grunge of Panama, everything has stopped.

I may be exaggerating, but it is a dramatic moment.

FEDERICO

Twenty-three

OBSESSION.

I think about him day and night, during classes, on the train, trying to figure out a way to see him again. Write about him at length in my diary. *No one like him in Dayton, no one who looks like him or talks like him* . . . I go on for pages about his face and manner: *his quiet calm and deadly serenity—a good deadly, exciting deadly.*

Of course I'm no longer sullen or morose. I'm thoughtful and conniving.

I've definitely entered the world of misdemeanors, because seeing him will have to be secret and that heightens my fever of stealth.

Grinding away at it constantly, I try to come up with an idea that will take me back to that cabin (or wherever he is), but days go by and I come up with nothing. He's slaving away in the Cut six days a week and I don't know where he is on Sundays. That's the day I'm with my family. My brain sizzles.

Nobody knows this is churning in me. I cover it well. School work continues—turned in on time, high marks. I know the trust and freedom that buys me.

I can't go to Father for help on this one. I'll have to get to Federico on my own.

I won't give up, of course. I'm obsessed.

Twenty-four

SUNDAY. A huge group of laborers is coming along the track toward our house. Mother and I are sitting on the porch and she watches them a minute. "Spanish, aren't they?" she says. We know the dress of different nationalities by now.

I'm suddenly alert. "Looks like it," I say. I don't see Federico among them. We watch them approach.

I've been hearing Father praise the Spanish all along, saying they're the real thing, genuine workers, stocky with strong shoulders. "Good boys. They can take directions and they're well liked, dependable. Heat doesn't bother them a bit and they're strong. I saw a Spanish fella put an iron cookstove on his shoulder and walk up a hill with it. Quartermaster's using them now, too. Every department wants them."

And there they are, these stocky Spanish workers, but no Federico. These are only desperate Spaniards from Cuba and Spain, rough peasants who found work on the canal when they couldn't get it at home. I can see there are several hundred of them, and they've come along the track from the north toward our house. They wear rope-soled cloth *alparagatos.* Some wear velvet berets and colorful sashes, their Sunday best.

"It looks like the entire Spanish work force," Mother says.

But still I don't see Federico, and when they're close, we see something strange. Every man is carrying a plate.

Mother says, "What do you suppose . . . ?"

They climb our hill and two of the men come to the door.

"El jefe," they say. They want the boss.

Father's wearing a robe, reading his paper in the living room. The fellows wait politely outside, berets in hand, while Father pulls on some clothes. He goes out and they exchange a few words. He takes a plate and examines it. He sniffs at it, frowns. He starts down the hill and the whole group follows.

They cross the track, go up the opposite hill to the dispensary, and gather around the steps while Father goes inside. After a few minutes Father comes out and speaks to the men. Mother and I can't hear what he says. The men nod and seem satisfied. We can hear *"gracias,"* and then they start down the track toward their barracks, all several hundred of them.

When Father comes back up the hill, he's disturbed. "Trying to feed them rotten meat."

He doesn't get agitated very often. But something has gone wrong. He respects his workers and won't tolerate careless abuse, and that is what has happened. "I won't get the smell of those plates out of my head for weeks."

He gives us the plate he's still carrying and Mother and I both take a whiff.

A rank smell, and Mother says, "Dear Lord," and sets it at a distance on the porch floor. Father has just become the Spaniards' protector and spokesman. They've been given bad meat and he's set things straight. Their American *jefe* goes back in to his Sunday paper, glad to be of help because abuse of power disturbs him.

But where's Federico? I'm disturbed because masses of Spanish men came to our door and he was not with them.

Then they come back the next week and again Federico isn't with them. But this time there is a payoff.

Twenty-five

IT'S THE FOLLOWING SUNDAY and another large delegation arrives —no Federico.

Up our hill they come again, several weeping women among them this time. Father goes out to hear their problem, which they explain in simple Spanish:

"Some of our boys went swimming in a water hole in the Cut. One of them crushed his head diving into a rock." The mother of the boy moans. The other women hold her close. "Now we're unable to bury the dead boy, *Jefe*, because there's no priest to officiate. What can we do?"

"But I'm no priest. How can I help?"

"We just need someone to read the words." None of them can read Latin.

There's silence and Father thinks it over. From my angle through the living-room window I see him pondering the propriety of reading the words of a priest. He's not a priest or even Catholic and doesn't know Latin. He looks down at the porch floor a long time, then says, "Leave the book, *deja el libro*." It's a prayer book of some kind. "I'll study it. We'll do it first thing in the morning."

I don't like this religious mumbo jumbo. There's no foreign language in our Methodist church. Just straightforward hell and damnation if you don't watch your step, and it's in plain English.

I go upstairs to my room, get back to work thinking how to corral Federico, and realize what an amateur I am at this boy/girl thing. I regret it for the first time.

The next morning, after an evening of coaching by Mother, Father slowly reads the Latin text; the Spaniards cross themselves, weep, and sometimes murmur, "Amen." And that's when it comes to me—at the moment of all the amens. I have the perfect plan.

How could I have missed thinking of it before? It's simple, uncomplicated, and almost on the up and up. I'm hugely relieved.

The solemn service is almost over and the women are weeping in grief, but my torment is at an end. I'm smiling.

From below come Father's last plaintive words: "... *in nomine Patris et Filii et Spiritus Sancti*. Amen."

Amen means "so be it," doesn't it?

Twenty-six

TWO DAYS LATER, AFTER DINNER, I put on jodhpurs and my regular jungle gear. I make a breezy announcement to Mother:

"I'm meeting Harry at the bottom of the hill. Going to Empire this time—he's enumerating over there now." A detail I add to make my story more believable. I'm lying, of course. I won't be meeting Harry this week at all—he's tending to other business, but Mother doesn't know that and I start toward the door.

She stops putting dishes in the cupboard and turns. She looks at me hard. "When is a nice young man from your school going to come here and call for you and take you out for the evening?"

I stop in my lying tracks. I don't have an answer and this isn't a rhetorical question; she wants a response. It's been bothering her. She wants to know why, at seventeen (I've just had a birthday), this nice-young-man thing isn't happening. Why am I still a tomboy in jodhpurs counting workers for the past half a year with the census taker and still enjoying it?

I look her in the eye and words come out of me I didn't know I had. I even have a slightly weary tone, as though explaining it again is just too much. I roll my eyes. (Where did that come from?)

"I'm writing about the Zone census for school, Mother. Nobody else is doing it."

Her eyes bore into me but I don't waver. I'm strong and I'm winning. First time in my life.

I'm shaking inside, but I know she's thinking about Mrs. Ewing's note and praise for my essays. Good, let her think about that. I also know that in her mind good grades are no substitute for finding a nice young man and having a well-rounded social life of some kind, any kind.

My words remind her that I'm the only student recorder of the census taking, a fact that annoys her but works. I see her wheels turning. She takes her time. She isn't uncomfortable in silence, but I am at the moment. I wait her out. *Think it over,*

Mother. There's no reason for me not to go out as usual. And then she speaks.

"Be careful," she says and slides a platter in between upright pegs on a shelf.

Unbelievable. It worked. I stood my ground and I'm free.

I duck out to the steps. Could I have done this a year ago? (If I could have, I would have.) But I don't waste time on the past or on the present small victory. I go on down the steps, and before I reach the tracks, I have to sit for a minute. I'm shaking. I'm breathless. Was any teen ever so restricted, so bound by obedience? After that little confrontation and bold fabrication, I feel myself smiling and I'm light as a feather, strong and free. I'm not afraid at all. I'm just shaking because what I did was risky. I'm a new person and it's a new world, and I don't mind that lying is nerve-racking.

Twenty-seven

I CROUCH ON THE STEPS UNTIL I SEE the last of the workers pass by, which is part of the plan. These are the men who plant dynamite in the trees to be cleared, an evening job. When they've gone by, I put on a slouched hat that I've scrounged from Father's closet and tuck up my hair. I'm taking a chance being out alone at night in the Zone, a girl by herself. But I'm no fool. I have a plan.

I complete dressing in my worker's gear and feel comfortable. I go down the last steps and begin making my way along the tracks in the darkness. I encounter the usual passersby—women balancing baskets on their heads, children scuttling around them, a single wordless worker hurrying along, one *borracho* weaving and humming to himself—I can't make out if he's American or a local. No one speaks to me—*great*—I keep my head down. My ruse is working. I may actually look a little threatening, which suits me fine. A small man, head down, wide-brimmed hat covering his face—I have the feeling they want nothing to do with me.

After a while I reach Federico's cabin and stop. Up the hill the light is on, but from below, the steep angle keeps me from seeing inside so I make my way closer from bush to bush, being careful to stay hidden. I find a large oleander and position myself behind it. I watch.

It's light inside. I hear voices and quiet conversation. Then I hear water. I make my way around to the back, find a hiding place, and see a figure in a makeshift shower—a bucket on a shelf tipped so that it pours water onto pieces of split bamboo, creating a dribbling stream. It's dark where I am and I move closer.

Federico is standing in the water washing himself, the light from inside the cabin flashing across his body, water sheeting off his skin, glossy. I don't move.

I stand hidden and watch the soap foam sliding down his arms and chest to his legs in the dark. His hair is wet and shiny, his arms and shoulders sunburned a dark brown. His hands slide into his armpits and across his chest—a beautiful, lean, powerful body. I don't move my eyes.

He replaces the emptied bucket with a full one, all this movement half obscured in the darkness, flashes of water on his arms and legs as he bends and lifts. The shower starts again, a stronger sprinkling of water, and he begins rinsing himself, swiping the water off his arms and chest with his hands, taking some careful time with the darkness between his legs, then standing straight and shaking his head like a dog.

The drops spray to the side, all this only half lit, flickering like a moviola. He takes a ragged but neatly folded towel from the sill of the window and wipes his face, runs it through his hair, and wraps it around his waist. He rests his hands on his hips and looks out at the night, standing still, a few drops of water from his hair on his shoulders, a few very dark hairs in the center of his chest drawn down by the stream of water running toward his navel, where the towel is tucked.

For a second he's looking directly at me. I hold my breath. My face is only half visible, his eyes on the foliage around me. Then he looks up to the sky and studies the stars, turns his body searching for the constellations. Another moment, then he looks in my direction again. I don't move, don't breathe. He reaches up, sets the two buckets upside down, and goes back into the cabin.

Two steps closer and I can see inside.

His head bobs when he pulls on thin cotton trousers with a drawstring at the waist, a kind of pajama. I work my way closer through the vines and bushes. I can see fully into the room, and I watch him sit at his table and begin writing. A letter, maybe, to his wife, his mother . . . a girlfriend? Jealousy ripples through me—some kind of turmoil does.

I realize a roommate is on the other cot, a young man his age. They don't talk, only go on with their reading and writing. Federico looks stern and unapproachable to me, and worldly. I don't think I'll ever be able to speak to him or know him.

I stare, watch him a long time with a mix of excitement and fear—surely he's off-limits for me. I'm a small-town girl.

He finishes writing, puts away the pen and paper, and starts reading. Something makes him smile. He reaches for the pen and writes on a notepad. He has a warm, inviting smile. Then he goes back to reading and he looks aloof again.

Bugs are biting me and it's hot; I have to move.

I go as quietly as I can to the side of the cabin and take another long look. The lights glow. I can see the two heads reading. Some raucous noise comes from the adjacent cabins—less literate workers playing cards, laughing, talking. When bugs start gnawing on me again, I move farther away through the brush, careful, noiseless, and make my way on down the hill to the track. From there I look back a last time and I can no longer see them sitting inside. They've disappeared behind the angle of the hill, and I can see only the top of the cabin roof. All this has taken ten, maybe twelve, minutes, no more.

I start walking fast toward our house, head down, hat pulled low. American women are not allowed out alone at night and I know it. Everything I'm doing is risky.

I pass a noisy dollar house where the workers are getting drunk on the ninety-proof jungle hooch they brag about. No liquor is sold in the Zone on Sundays, and there's no gambling ever. I shouldn't even see all this. At night those laws must be lax. I wonder how the men can get up at four thirty after hard drinking like that, but of course the thought doesn't stick. All I can see is Federico's hand sweeping the water off his body—particularly the glistening drops on the darkness below his belly, almost lost in the shadows.

I've never seen Father naked except when he's scurrying from the bathroom to the bedroom, which is nothing like what I've just seen—the flashing movements of Federico in the jungle darkness, his muscular shoulders and strong back, nakedness clothed in shadows. I'm simmering, but then, everything simmers in Panama. It's hot, it's humid, and I'm all that.

"That was quick," Mother says when I walk in. It shocks me as though she woke me from a dream, then I remember that Harry and I are always out for half the night.

"I forgot," I say. "I have to get up early and collect leaves for a botany assignment. Harry walked me back."

"Mmm," she says.

This latest lie is not nerve-racking. I'm getting better at it.

I go past her fast, thinking surely she'll see something different about me, but she doesn't.

She says, "Sleep well," the way she always does, and I go up to my room raging with guilt and erotic excitement. I play the scene of Federico in the shower over and over in my mind as I climb into bed. There I write about it in great detail, my diary my one and only confidant. My handwriting is larger, looser. It's because I'm still a little breathless, but I decide it means something—I don't know what. I'm excited and unable to sleep, my body different, feeling different to me.

I get to know it, this new electric body of mine, accompanied by Federico's wonderful flashing image. A memorable night.

Next morning I make sure my diary is well hidden, remember that the payoff for lying is worth the risk, then my thoughts go back to Federico.

Now What?

Twenty-eight

THE FOLLOWING SUNDAY: A BEAUTIFUL DAY, bright sunshine, a good breeze. I put on my best white dress and carry a parasol like a "lady" and I'm ready for the Tivoli family picnic.

"Very nice," says Mother. She must think I'm giving up my tomboy ways. Normally I would object to the dress (it's tight in the waist and bodice) and to white shoes, but no, I've cleaned the shoes without her asking and don't object to the dress. She has no idea why.

The park in front of the Tivoli Hotel is filled when we get there. The thirty-six-piece Isthmian Canal Commission Band is on the platform looking smart in white, playing their popular tunes: "Moonlight Bay," "Alexander's Ragtime Band." I'm not listening. I have a job: search the crowd for Federico's face. That's the reason for the dress and parasol and spotless shoes.

He will surely be there. Everyone is—school friends, their

families, all the bosses and engineers, Colonel Goethals himself. He's chief engineer, head of the Commission. He never misses a function—white suit, shock of white hair, the boss of everyone.

Dr. and Mrs. Gorgas show up—he's the one who got malaria under control with quinine squads and oil gangs spraying pools and puddles long before we arrived. Marie Gorgas comes over to Mother.

"It's good to see you," she says. "When are you coming to visit?"

They were both teachers and have common school friends in the States. It's natural they should get together, become Zone friends, but Mother is very uncomfortable in social situations.

"Very soon, I promise," she says, but she'll find a way out, she always does. She'll put it off so long, it will be forgotten—standard operating procedure for her—and then she'll be free of the whole thing. Meanwhile they chat nicely and I continue searching the crowd.

I check people behind trees, sitting on blankets, walking arm in arm. I stare at tables and walk through the crowd on my own, leaving Mother and Father with their friends.

I fold my parasol, uncomfortable to encounter Federico decorated in a frilly dress that isn't really me. But it's better than being caught dressed as a man hiding behind his oleander bush. I haven't entirely kicked the tomboy demeanor but I do want to look good, like a pretty girl somehow. I stand very straight, as though that counts for something. I station myself at the edge of the gazebo.

The annoying tunes thump overhead. The band plays "Wait 'til the Sun Shines, Nellie." Children dodge through adults, and occasionally the loudspeaker announces one of them lost or calls out the name of the next event. This could be Dayton. But it's not.

I tick off each man's face—methodical, thorough—and then it hits me: Federico isn't here. He couldn't be.

Twenty-nine

HE'S A LABORER. How did I make this mistake? What was I thinking, or not thinking?

Federico can walk around town or even around the hotel, but he can't participate in this traditional Sunday gathering. He's a pick-and-shovel man. He and those like him have their place, and it's not here among the golden Americans in their weekend merrymaking.

This occasion is for skilled engineers and bosses and their families—Zoners. No diggers in this bunch. Harry can be here but not Federico. So can Father and shovel engineer Ned, who's already drunk and getting loud, but not Federico, even with his head full of philosophies and several languages and a face more European and excellent than anyone else's. *No laborer is allowed at these functions except to serve.* Where is my brain?

(I wonder if my risky night watching the Spaniard displaced my logic. I really wonder about that.)

I tell myself this could have happened to anybody in a haze of infatuation and hope I'm not becoming as dizzy as the girls at school. The blare of the band overhead is making me crazy.

I go to a cluster of trees where people have picnics spread on the ground and stretch out on the grass. I stare up through feathery leaves and doze off. No doubt the nap is some form of escape from the afternoon's embarrassing disappointment, but I wake up with something useful. A new plan and a good one. I know (think I know) it will work.

I'll provide Federico with books.

I look up in the sky and smile, unburdened, determined not to be overenthusiastic with this scheme. I'll consider each step, think it through, and proceed carefully. No dressing up like a man. No wild goose chase. Just this very sensible idea, and all I have to do is encounter him again, run into him, and I can do that. Somehow.

First, the books. *Books.*

Thirty

"I'LL GET YOU SOMETHING YOU'LL LIKE," says the Zone librarian with a wink. She has no idea. It's the next morning and I want her to stay out of my business, but I smile and wait.

She comes back with a novel by Mary Roberts Rinehart, *When a Man Marries.* (I'm a magnet for this kind of misguided thinking. My age, maybe?)

"That's not quite it," I say. "I'm actually here for someone else. Could I browse?"

"I suppose so," she says, but she's not happy. I've threatened her librarian skills.

She allows me behind the desk and leads me to new books not yet shelved. They're stacked on the floor in a random manner. It's cool down there so I sit and go through them, taking my time, but twice the librarian has to step over me. I'm underfoot.

I begin shuffling through the stack faster and it's not promising: romance novels, mysteries, detective stories, adventures, espionage tales, a disaster book, biographies, a family saga, fantasies, an autobiography, a book on African wildlife, a new translation of the Bible (how 'bout that?), something on motorcycles, a comical farce with "Sure to Leave You Weeping with Laughter" ribboned across the front, then . . . *The Interpretation of Dreams.* Ah.

I've never heard of it, but Dr. Freud sounds scholarly enough. And German. I riffle through the pages. Nonfiction—perfect.

I take it to the checkout desk. The librarian looks shocked, then disapproving. I look her straight in the face and don't falter, not for a second. I have no time for this nonsense.

"Due in two weeks," she says. Stamp!

I'm out of there.

Thirty-one

DOWN THE TRACK I GO TOWARD FEDERICO'S CABIN, the Freud book in hand. (I have every right to take a walk after school.)

I'm heated but more with excitement this time, not the temperature, which is at its dry-season, midafternoon peak. The sun is merciless and when I get to Federico's cabin my dress is streaked with perspiration. Still, it doesn't bother me.

From the tracks I can see the flaps are rolled up to let in fresh air while he and his roommate are working. It's a Wednesday. Because I remember Harry saying something about a day off in the middle of the week, I'm hopeful. ("It's for workers who plant dynamite after regular hours." "What's the requirement to plant dynamite?" "Good sense, I suppose. They put it in the tree trunks, then run like hell.")

I wait for Federico on the cabin steps, hoping he'll show up.

Trains clatter by. I try to read but the heat is blistering.

I'm ready with my story. I'll tell him I found a book I thought might interest him—I saw his books when I was there with the census taker, does he remember? I'll sound businesslike, friendly but not silly. The key is to act casual, as though the whole thing is an afterthought.

Sweat drips on the book.

More trains pass.

The sun is relentless.

I'm that sizzling ant under the magnifying glass. It bakes me, and finally I realize he'll be coming back as usual on the 5:30 labor train with all the other workers and I have to be home by then. Another stupid mistake I've made. I give up.

I take a last look at the cabin and start home. The heat is scorching, and this time with the excitement drained out of me, I'm bothered.

When I walk into the kitchen Mother pours me a lemonade and gives me a strange look.

"You're soaked," she says. "What happened?"

"Um . . . y'know . . ." I shrug.

She drops it.

That night I try to think clearly, to come up with a foolproof way to meet Federico, but I can't. I'm failing for lack of imagination. Maybe it's over and all I'll ever have is that glimpse of him in the shower at night, which is a lot, but in the long run it's only a jungle adventure and it will fade. I'll eventually forget it. With that dark thought very clearly in mind, I go to sleep.

I go unconscious, actually, because I've given up. I've surrendered. Sleep is escape again and I don't care if I ever wake up.

Thirty-two

THE OLD DAYTON WAYS ARE ROOTED DEEP.

I do wake up, of course, but I'm depressed and realize immediately I have to snap out of it, regroup, not give up. Nothing is accomplished by giving up. The Wrights had tons of failure and they didn't give up. That's how they learned what didn't work—failure is the path to success. I get a grip and realize I've been doing it right all along. I've been eliminating what doesn't work and I have to keep going—stay with it and use what I've learned from past mistakes.

Deep breath—I feel better. But there's nobody to talk to about this and thrash it out. Can't talk to the girls at school and not my parents. I'm on my own. Only my diary hears about this, and that's not a conversation. Trying to come up with a way to encounter Federico sounds simple, but it isn't. He works twelve grueling hours a day, six days a week, and I'm at school and expected home by four. Still, I'm convinced it can be done, and by midmorning in English class, I'm optimistic. I hear Mrs. Ewing's voice:

". . . and include as much geology as possible."

What did she say just before that? Something about a new essay assignment: what your father does on the canal. She's written it on the board.

This is pure annoyance. I have no time for this kind of thing, going for half a day with Father into the Cut to watch what he does, think about it, write about it, which is what she wants. I know it's important and he does it well, but I don't want to give it any time or thought. Time and thought are the things I use for solving my Federico problem. I'm angry. At school, at Mrs. Ewing, at her assignment.

I resolve to make it into something useful. I will be in the Cut and there are workers down there, tens of thousands of them, actually, and among them somewhere Federico. Could he really take a few moments, lean on his shovel, and chat with me about Freud between ton-loosening blasts? Of course, I'd have to find him first.

The day arrives and I join Father, all this an annoying distraction. I'm sullen. He doesn't notice my mood. He loves having me come along, but I've been in the Cut before and I'm not interested —I just want to get it over with.

Mother and I have gone with him on a Sunday down the long stairs with other families and stood gawking at the immensity. But today, for my assignment, Father will tell me about it again. He'll include more detail and he'll love every minute.

One excellent thing: I get to wear my out-with-Harry clothes—no skirts allowed in the Cut during working hours.

Maybe because of that and Father's enthusiasm I actually do forget about Federico . . . for a short time.

So I stand with Father early in the morning and he plunges in, gestures toward the various machines and work sectors: ". . . midnight supply trains bring in coal for the shovels . . ." I take notes. ". . . they're kept running twenty-four hours, eighty-five of them running at any given time." Impressive. "Blasters send down rocks and the diggers go to work breaking them up. The shovelers move in and put eight tons of boulders and dirt onto a car in a single bite. My job is to keep those cars running and carry the spoil away . . ."

How could I take this lightly? I'm impressed all over again. I like the mechanics, the nuts and bolts of how things work. Got that, no doubt, from working with the boys and from Father— genes don't discriminate much by gender.

And something else. Down inside the canal with the workers, it's different from a Sunday stroll there with Zoner families. That's a sightseeing tour, benign and touristy. In the sweat and noise of a workday there's a frightening aspect, a looming threat, as if the whole thing might decide to swallow us, then spit us out, like a gargantuan serpent fed up with the relentless grinding on its gut. It makes me uneasy.

Not Father, though. He's in his element. He's calm and happy, hard at work. He keeps talking and I write as fast as I can.

He points to the trackshifter. (Yet again.) The giant mantis is parked as usual by the wall, waiting.

"Every night it repositions the rails—picks them up and lays them down in a new spot. Have to move the whole operation along, tracks and all . . ."

I think it's the humanness of the machine that gets him, the way it behaves like a child with a train set, rearranging the track at will, easily. It's a giant human. But aren't all machines? I'll make that part of the essay, what giant machines do. How like us they are, the trackshifter with its giant arms and giant prehensile claw. It's all we know, our puny human bodies, so we copy them and make machines. This is the kind of thing that gets me top marks and I know it.

I glance around at the workers, pick-and-shovel fellows, glistening in the heat. I want to have a word with them. But Father goes on talking and I write and boulders crash onto flatcars, steam shovels grind, and warning whistles scream before every blast. I think I can't take much more, then Father finishes speaking and stands thoughtful in the deafening inferno. I have to ask him:

"Doesn't the bedlam wear you out?"

"Noise means it's progressing the way it's supposed to. Doesn't bother me a bit."

That's why he's boss, I think, and make note of that, too.

"I need a break," I tell him.

"Sure."

I make my way across dirt clods and gullies to a group of workers, scores of them that line the canal wall breaking up the larger boulders. There's just a chance . . .

"Hay Castellanos aquí?" I say.

"No. *Antillano solo.*" No Spanish, only West Indians.

I look on down the length of the canal. As far as I can see there are workers, forty thousand of them at any given time. I've just queried a dozen and Federico is not among them. This is folly.

I take a good look at the canal, a rare view from the floor, and finish off my notes: shovels are stacked one above the other; seven different levels; seven parallel tracks, moved to new positions every day; dirt trains moving back and forth with no snarls. This is my father's job, overseeing all this.

I'm done, or think I am. But then something remarkable happens.

Thirty-three

FROM THE CORNER OF MY EYE I SEE THE IMPOSSIBLE. I take a good look. A steam shovel is sinking.

There's no doubt about it—the shovel is sinking. A barely perceptible movement.

I nudge Father. "Look."

He's busy, doesn't respond.

I poke him again. "Look!"

He turns his head. Shovel number forty-nine is sinking.

Father's jaw drops. Seconds pass. The shovel lowers and we watch. Blasting noise continues around us.

Father calls over to another engineer and he, too, watches, all of us in disbelief. The shovel descends, still swinging eight-ton buckets of dirt to a waiting railcar, both engineers on board totally unaware.

Several pick-and-shovel workers now see the phenomenon and call out to fellow workers, *"Mira! Mira este . . ."* and there's minor panic.

Workers drop their tools. They back off, spooked. We all are. It couldn't be happening. The steam shovelers notice, too, and suddenly stop, which signals all the other workers and everything comes to a halt.

Now, behind us, a railcar pulls up and Colonel Gaillard hops off and comes striding forward with great authority—he's our lead construction engineer. "Ah, you've seen it."

"What's going on?" says Father.

"It's happening all along the Cut, about a foot a minute, all morning."

"What is it?"

"We're rising." He waves toward the canal center. "We're on soft strata here in the middle so the slides along the walls are pushing us up. The shovels aren't sinking—they're near the wall. We're rising."

Father looks over the situation and sees that what Gaillard says is true. "How far will it go?" he asks him.

"We don't know. But it's nothing to worry about."

He's never seen such a thing. Nobody has. Nobody's ever done anything like this before, so everything is new. How does he know it's nothing to worry about?

Gaillard goes back to his transport car. He sits observing the phenomenon until it stops. Then he gives Father a little salute and he's on his way.

Can-do Americans—there's no stopping them.

Father calls out to the workers that everything is okay, to go back to work. They trust him. Pick-and-shovel men begin swinging their tools. Steam shovelers give their idling engines a throaty roar and everything resumes. Tons of lava rock blast to the canal floor and shovels deposit the tons into a waiting railcar. My father is boss of that. That's what he does in the canal.

Thirty-four

AT SUPPER FATHER KNIFES THE AIR WITH HIS HAND.

"Like pressing down on the side of a pan of dough—the dough will push up in the middle. The slides on the sides of the canal are making the soft floor in the middle rise. It has nowhere else to go."

"Terrible," Mother says.

"No, only the slides are terrible. We may never stop them."

"What then?"

"We keep digging."

Father keeps saying these words and it disturbs me. I don't want to think of everything moving forward while my dilemma remains—his success to my failure. The work goes on in spite of slides and yet I can't reach Federico. I might never see him again.

"We'll dredge when it's full of water if we have to," Father says. "That's what matters—keep going, keep working. Gaillard and Goethals, you never see them shaken. Canal center rising—they're calm, tell us to wait till it stops and then go on. Nobody's ever seen anything like it, but we do as we're told and we're fine. Most important thing—attitude and endurance."

It's important, all right, and it's admirable, but to me it's disturbing.

Father takes a bite of beefsteak. All's well in his world.

I include Father's remarks in the essay and my own remarks about machines made in our likeness. A few days later I get the highest grade in class and an extra nod from Mrs. Ewing. I stare out the window and don't hear anything more she says. A student starts reading: "My father's work in the Cut . . ."

I can't bear to listen. I have bigger problems—I may never see Federico again (that dark feeling is back). I know where he lives and I have no excuse to go there. It's simple. It's not a question of attitude or endurance or even of learning from failure. I'm failing again for lack of imagination and my positive attitude is gone. I've lost hope, this time for good. Horse sense is telling me I won't see Federico again and it's a fact I'd better accept.

I sit in class hot, bored, and numb.

MUCHAS GRACIAS, DR. FREUD
Thirty-five

WE MEET IN FRONT OF THE TIVOLI!

Luck. Pure luck.

It's early one evening, Mother's inside the hotel, and I'm sitting on a bench reading *The Interpretation of Dreams*. It's tough going and I'm concentrating, probably frowning. I turn back a page to reread something and realize there are rope-soled shoes in front of me. They're at a respectful distance but definitely pointed toward me—the shoes of a Spanish worker. A voice says, "Pardon," and I look up.

It's Federico.

He's dressed in clean clothes, politely holding his beret in front of him. I'm completely calm (and aware that I'm calm), and I can see he doesn't remember me. He's thinking—probably about approaching me, and the book, and what to say. Then his expression changes and he does remember. He smiles and looks relieved.

"Ah. You were with the enumerator."

"Yes."

"I'm sorry to bother you. I noticed what you're reading . . . Did you get the book here?" My plan is working! Weeks of thinking about him, conniving to meet him, dreaming of him day and night, giving up hope, and now he's standing in front of me and wants to know where the book came from. The book!

"It's from the American library. Here, take it." I hold it out to him. I'm calm and bold.

"No, no, no, no . . . I only wanted to know where you got it."

"The library. Go on, take it. You'll be doing me a favor."

"I only want—"

"Take it. Really." I hold the book toward him again and he sees I mean it. "It's a little over my head. Read it and tell me what you think." I lightly touch his hand with the edge of the book. "Please." (I amaze myself.)

Federico takes the book. He opens it, scans the pages, and eases onto the bench beside me, totally absorbed. I feel the warmth of his body next to me and then there's his scent—the soap used in Panama. He's been in the shower. The shower. Concentrate.

"I have a Tolstoy at home," I say. *The Death of Ivan Ilych.*

He looks up quickly. "A beautiful story."

"Do you want it?"

"Well . . ." Hard for him to resist.

"I can get almost anything. I put in a request and it comes on the next boat. Just tell me what you want." I shrug at the simplicity of it and don't care at all if he knows what I'm doing, that I'm making myself available and attractive to him. But really it's the books that interest him. I know that.

He smiles. He's got to be astonished at this piece of luck—an evening like the others, when he's walking along, and what comes into his view but Dr. Freud's book, which he must know about and want but doesn't have a prayer of getting. "You're too generous," he says.

"Not at all. I'm always at the library . . ." I smell the wool of his beret. (Wool in Panama!)

"Yes. Then, yes," he says. I've changed his life in half a minute. "I won't keep it long."

"Keep it as long as you want."

I've got to revel in this—it's too good to be true. And I'm so calm; where did that come from?

He starts talking about what books he wants, but I'm drifting and hear only the clipped English accent, and I relax in the closeness of him. I am myself. I don't think I've ever been myself before, not like this. He's talking about books, of course, and he's enthusiastic and at ease, not like he was when Harry and I first saw him so cool and aloof in his cabin. I picture him in his makeshift shower, enjoy visualizing that awhile, then his voice comes back.

". . . Melville . . . I haven't read all of him. And Rousseau and the French classics, of course . . ." He's holding the Freud, gesturing with it, and suddenly he stops. "I'm sorry, I'm running on."

"No, you're not. I don't have anybody to talk to about books— I love it."

Another smile and then it turns awkward. Our little exchange is suddenly finished—no place to go with it unless he wants me to rattle on about Dayton.

"Well . . ." he says. He stands, a gentleman ready to take his leave, formal again and proper.

The Freud is folded in his arm against his chest. He stands there like a character from an English novel, ready to bid me adieu. Then (I don't know why I do it) I break the spell.

"This'll be fun," I say, light and easy. Wait, yes, I do know why. I'm creating an ongoing relationship and it *will* be fun.

He has to laugh a little. "Yes, it will."

He doesn't know what else to say and neither do I.

I think he's as happy as I am.

"Our book exchange," I say, giving it a name, lest he forget what we're establishing here.

He looks at me with curiosity for a few seconds, and I hope he's seeing something more than the seventeen-year-old daughter of an engineer, who he must suppose is a spoiled American, part of the mob.

Trusting he's seeing more than that, I say, "They'll think I'm a genius at the library, such a prolific reader." Another chuckle between us. (Cripes, I'm good at this.) "Promise to tell me what you think." I nod toward the Freud.

"Of course."

He gives the book a wiggle in the air, then a little bow from the waist and he turns away.

He walks into the crowd hugging the Freud close like a professor. I watch until he's disappeared.

Thirty-six

I BREATHE DEEP AND LOOK AROUND.

The hotel must have installed extra lights, because everything looks brighter and the people are better looking than I remember, or maybe I'm just noticing things. Maybe the hotel lights are stronger—that could be it. But everything really is light and bright, the whole world, everything, everybody. The white clothes everyone wears makes them glow, and the kids running around seem exceptionally smart all of a sudden—bright, intelligent kids these Zoners have. Everything shimmers.

It's peaceful, too. And so am I. (They must have put in more lights.)

That night I picture Federico at his desk reading the Freud. I see him talking to his roommate about how he got the book, the coincidental meeting, the girl who was with the enumerator dropping into his life again from the sky.

I picture him at his desk taking notes, reading with one foot propped on the other chair and later reading on his cot and falling asleep, the book open on his chest—I can't close my eyes thinking about it. My diary entry is brief: *Met him at Tivoli.* I'll add to that later. Maybe not. That says it all. I feel so alive, I never want to drift off. Our meeting runs through my mind over and over.

I try to imagine how we look to others, how we sound when

we talk. Endless scenarios. Brief encounters, long ones, all of them easy and comfortable, like the meeting in front of the hotel. We're kindred souls. I'm convinced of it.

The next morning I get up without a minute of sleep feeling refreshed and full of energy. My life has direction and I'm not alone; Federico is in it.

Surely there's nothing I can't accomplish.

Simply put: there's nothing I can't do.

Thirty-seven

HARRY AND I TAKE THE 10:10 TRAIN TO GATUN, the town by the dam site. He has to do his enumerating there because much of the territory is going to be covered by water. Mother says I should go with him and see what's about to disappear forever—part of the learning experience, she harps on. I'm happy to do it but I have my own agenda.

We sit in a half-empty passenger car. The wooden seats are polished and lacquered, silver metal fittings everywhere, the glass windows sparkling clean. The Panama Railroad is a model of efficiency, no doubt about it, and it's always on schedule. Our train slips out of the station at ten past, exactly.

Harry is my tutor in politics, geography, and language, whether he knows it or not. He points out the villages on the way.

"Matachin, named for a Chinese man who killed himself. That's what they tell the tourists."

"Sounds like a play on words to me," I say. "*Mata*, 'kill'; *chin* for 'Chinese.' Probably Indian, don't you think? Some ancient glyph on a rock somewhere?"

"Probably." He gives me a sidelong look. "You're good with language, you know that?" I look away, embarrassed. That's a big compliment coming from Harry. Federico wafts through my brain.

Bas Obispo rolls by.

Jungle after that.

We go through Gorgona, the Pittsburgh of the Zone, acres of machine shops working on some of Father's tracks and engines, Federico's face and words doing a lot of wafting at this point. Then we go through stations that are small and wasting away: Bailamonos and San Pablo and Orca L'garto. Harry knows them all and points them out. I take notes and sketch.

"Tabernilla—look," he says. What used to be a village is now stacks of lumber being loaded on flatcars. "Moving it toward the Pacific, they'll build it again."

The same thing is happening in Frijoles when we pass it— dismantling, loading, moving the entire town with every- thing from police station to homes, five years after founding it. Creating, destroying, re-creating on higher ground, whatever it takes to build the canal. Make way for the encroaching waters of man-made Lake Gatun. Already the jungle vines and foliage are crawling in, taking over the one-time towns, and soon man's visit will be sunk deep by progress. At least, that's the plan, and it's not likely to go wrong.

I write this in my notes, not to please Mother but for my new self: the injustice and inevitability and helplessness of the locals being warned and moved and warned again, stripped of planting grounds, of dwellings, village communities split and scattered to make way for progress. Harry teaches me well.

It is beginning to get to me, even while I concentrate on Federico and my new world with him.

"It'll all be flooded," Harry says. "They're closing the Gatun spillway in February."

"Will these tracks be under water?"

"Tracks, railway, all of it on the bottom of the lake. Steamers will be gliding over those palm trees and mangoes and big ferns. They'll all still be standing in the water, ships steaming back and forth over them until they die."

"That's eerie."

"Yeah."

An hour and we don't see the canal, only jungle and the occasional group of huts, then we burst out of the growth and onto the lake. The water is licking at the rails under us. The Zone city of Gatun is on the hillside, to my left the locks and the dam. I don't bother sketching—it'll be there for a long time. So will the station we're sliding into; it's stone, not meant to be moved. It's permanent and out of reach of the flood, built to stay. We get out, look around.

"You know when your train leaves?" he asks. (Always the good uncle.)

"Yes, I'm fine."

This is where Harry and I split up. I plan to go back without him.

"Be careful."

"I will."

His questionnaire ready, he goes to the laborers lined up at a station window for their paychecks—yet another way of reaching them for enumerating. I go to see the locks as Mother has instructed.

She doesn't know my real plan.

Thirty-eight

I WAS THERE THE YEAR BEFORE WITH FATHER but the change is enormous. *Gigantic* is a better word.

It's nearing the end of construction, and the size is so monstrous, it looks like aliens landed and tried to dwarf their machines to fit planet Earth but didn't manage to shrink them enough.

There's a giant aerial tramway swinging buckets of concrete to sky-high steel forms. These are for uprights that stand hundreds of feet in the air. And inside the unfinished walls I can see an enormous bull wheel lying on its side. I've read about that, and Mrs. Ewing has talked about it. That bruiser will open and shut the lock gates—Tinkertoys for God's children.

The gates themselves are half completed and look out of proportion, they're already so big, thousands of cubic feet of poured concrete soaring into the sky. Dazzling.

It comes together for the first time how the whole thing will work—the course of the Chagres River altered and hundreds of acres of land inundated because it's easier to float over the lava rock than blast through it. Blasting is necessary only in Culebra where Father's working and the mountains are so high, no lake can rise above them. It all makes sense. It's a perfect plan.

The colossal scale of it moves me. My eyes tear; my chest swells. I've been pretty disinterested up to now, but spread out before me like that, seeing what puny humans with their invented machines have done, I'm overwhelmed.

This is relentless will and endurance, the stuff of Goethals and Stevens before him. The tough, commanding majesty of it gets to me and, any injustice to locals aside, I'm staggered. It's a match for continental drift, and man didn't take centuries to do it.

I take notes, do sketches, see everything I can, then get back to business. My business. Federico.

I hurry to the station and catch an early train. I have to be back in Culebra by midafternoon to carry out my newest scheme.

Thirty-nine

ON THE TRAIN I SIT ALONE AT A WINDOW LOOKING OUT, antsy. Everything moves too slowly for me now in this new life with Federico.

I want to be where I'm going, do what I mean to do, with no waiting or delays. A long train trip, days at school, endless social gatherings, are tedious. Life is tedious unless it's oriented toward Federico, and here I am stuck on a slow train. It isn't really slow, of course. There are stops, which makes the trip feel long.

I take out a letter from Dayton. Mother says it has news from Katharine that will interest me.

I read: The boys are occupied with patents, no longer solving problems of aerodynamics. (This seems remote, like some other lifetime.) Nine years since that first flight and they're dealing with patents and inaccurate statements and tangled misinformation about their work. There are more issues of a mechanical nature, dates and misconstrued facts, all business and law, no more inventing. Poor Wil. Poor Orville. Glad I'm gone—the fun's over.

"The flying machine is challenged everywhere," Katharine writes, "copied with reckless impunity." She says their discoveries are not completely protected and "they've given up on the president and the secretary of war. They can't be convinced a flying machine is practical for defense and the government doesn't want to invest in it." I want to care about this but I can't. "The boys have to keep the Army rejection under covers since it will make negotiations with other governments difficult." I can see that problem but I can't see them dealing with it. No tinkering? No experiments? No adventure? All is not smooth in Dayton. It may be as complicated and slow there as my life in Panama.

Through Tabernilla again. Flatcars with lumber move in the opposite direction, the town being carried away.

Katharine says Wil wrote from Paris: "Been to the Louvre. Liked da Vinci's *John the Baptist* better than his *Mona Lisa*." Just like Wil to see a painting through his own eyes and not accept some critic's impression. No matter where he goes, he's his own man, has his own thoughts. That much hasn't changed. "A sign of character," Mother says. "Not going along with the herd."

We pull into Culebra station. I put away the letter. It's still early afternoon and my plan is on schedule. I start walking but I don't head for home. As I walk, I question my strategy:

Is this the right thing to do? *For my purposes it is.*

Is there a better way to get what I want? *Possibly.*

Is this even smart? *What difference does it make? It's the best idea I have.*

Would I do it again if necessary? *Sure.*

Forty

I WALK ALONG THE TRACK TOWARD FEDERICO'S CABIN. Mother won't expect me for another hour. I'll drop off books for him—simple enough, except that he's not expecting me. We haven't set up this type of exchange. It's a delivery.

For weeks we've been meeting on Sundays at some designated spot—my new secret life. It's actually innocent enough. I show the usual respect for my parents, do excellent schoolwork, and meet Federico regularly with books. Sometimes we meet at the Tivoli in the evening. Sometimes below our house at the bottom of the steps—a daring exchange before supper.

But it's always friendly—we say a few polite words, then he moves on. This delivery to his cabin is something new and personal. I wonder how he'll take it. I want to reach him where he lives, that was the real reason for going to Gatun with Harry.

Mother, without knowing it, suggested the whole thing. She

made it possible. "You have to see that area before it's flooded," she said. I agreed, knowing I'd have to change my schedule for one day, which is exactly what I needed.

Trudging along the track in midafternoon heat, I hear a single locomotive engine behind me coming at high speed; I know a fast-moving engine is the Zone's ambulance. If the worker inside is dead, he goes to the morgue; only injured, he'll go to the hospital. He might even recover.

The engine speeds by and I glimpse three workers with the engineer, all of them bent over an injured body. One of the workers is Federico.

Forty-one

I STOP WALKING AND STARE.

A hundred yards ahead, below Federico's cabin, the engine comes to a stop and the men lift the body out. As the engine pulls away, they carry it up the steps, an awkward business; nobody notices me watching from down the track. I creep closer. The men have finally managed to get the body up and into the cabin.

At the bottom of the steps I don't know what to do. I want to see in the cabin but it's too risky. I won't have an opportunity like this again soon and I can't bring myself to abandon my plan, so I decide to at least get a look. I start up the steps, books for Federico in my arms, stretching my neck to get a glimpse. I can hear intense voices. A few steps higher I can actually see in.

A dead body. I've never seen one before.

The man is lying on Federico's cot, his face half blown away. Part of his arm is missing and some of it hangs by flesh or splintered bone—it's hard to tell which. He's mangled, mutilated, dirt-blackened, and bloodied. I stare.

They're trying to clean him, but his clothes are ripped to carboned shreds and the bone is bare and glutinous with gore. The dangling arm makes him look like Marat in his bath but with half a face.

They stop talking or trying to repair the body any more, and there's silence. I stay still, crouching on the steps looking in. Two of them sit on the empty bed, and Federico kneels beside the dead man and lowers his head onto the edge of the cot. I think he's going to pray, which surprises me for some reason, but he doesn't. He weeps.

His shoulders shake.

I don't move. No one in the cabin does, either. Minutes pass.

Death by premature explosion—it happens all the time and it has to be what I'm looking at. Reports are in the paper every few days:

> At the Culebra storehouse a porter gets impatient with opening a box of dynamite and tries to knock off the cover with a machete—three men blown away.

> A dozen men killed in the Cut when they tap a clogged charge to get it in position.

Five killed and eight wounded when a tooth on shovel number 210 hits the cap of an unexploded charge.

Nineteen dead and forty injured at Bas Obispo—that one in the *Canal Record* this morning. And now death from dynamite in front of my eyes.

A hand comes down on my shoulder. I stand up so fast, I fall off balance.

A Zone policeman catches my arm and steadies me.

"What are you doing here?"

"I saw trouble; I thought I should help . . ."

"Do you know these people?"

"Not exactly . . ."

"Then go on home. You shouldn't be here at all." I hesitate and this burly fellow gives me a hard look. "Don't wander around this area."

"All right." I can't think of anything else to say and I go down the steps.

The policeman watches and I start along the track toward home, still carrying books meant for Federico. He keeps watching so I can't turn back.

All I wanted was to talk to Federico, and now what I've seen has changed everything. Something has happened to him, and I wonder if it changed us. I don't know who the dead man is, but he has to be important to Federico. They allowed him to take him in the cabin before going to the morgue. I don't know what I'll say about it or if I should say anything or even admit I was there. I've never seen a man sob, or a dead man, or mutilation.

I walk home, wipe my dripping face.

Forty-two

MOTHER KNOWS HARRY'S IN GATUN FOR A FEW MORE DAYS, SO I have no excuse for getting back to the cabin, but I'm on fire. I'm emboldened by the strange near encounter at Federico's cabin.

The next evening when she's not in the room, I put on Father's hat, a pair of trousers, and walk out the back door, down the steps to the tracks, and resolve to think of an excuse later . . . sketching . . . silhouettes for art class . . . constellations for science . . . whatever . . .

I'm bristling with excitement. I like it but it's risky.

I have to remember that Federico doesn't know what I saw. Everything between us is the same as far as he knows. Popping up at his cabin like I'm going to do is different, and given what I've seen, I'd say meeting him at a regular place, like the Tivoli, would be much better, but I can't make myself wait.

Cut loose on my own, I walk fast along the tracks, books for Federico under my arm, no parental constraints, making my own rules.

Approaching Federico's cabin I stop and reconsider. He doesn't expect me. Our meetings before this have always been planned and strictly business, exchanging one or two books he's read for new ones he wants. This time it will be different because it's unplanned, and that's where it gets tricky, because he has to be still grieving.

But I don't even consider going back.

My plan is to act as though I know nothing and show up with books.

Forty-three

HALFWAY UP THE STEPS I CAN SEE IN: Federico sitting at the table reading, the roommate on his bunk. The place is spotless. You'd never know this was a death scene—no blood, not even stains. *How did he do that?* And no disarray.

I climb the last steps to the door and tap. Both of them look up. The roommate squints at me.

"Could I see Federico?" I say, an American girl in a man's clothes, almost dark. "I'm sorry to bother you . . ."

"No, no. Come in." Federico has recognized me.

The roommate pushes open the door and Federico pulls out a chair.

I put the books on the table. He's calm with a slightly puzzled look, and I'm rattled far more than I expected. This is hard, showing up like this with no warning.

"Two more," I say, meaning the books. "I came by yesterday but I saw . . . you know . . ."

I've blurted it out. I didn't mean to do that.

"Ah," he says, calm, unaffected.

"Actually, I need to get the poetry from you," I say, which is true. I need the book for a school assignment.

My face feels like it's on fire. This is a huge mistake—everything is wrong and inappropriate. Yesterday, a dead man was lying a foot from where I'm standing, and now I'm talking about "Whitman, for school . . . I have to do a report . . ." Can he see I'm shaking?

In a normal voice he says, "Of course," and bends down and

starts going through books stacked on the floor. "That's Augusto," he says, meaning the roommate. "She's my source for books," he says to him in Spanish.

Augusto stands and shakes my hand. His face is intelligent, and he's got the stocky shape Father talks about that's common with Spanish workers—nothing like Federico's lean build.

"My pleasure," I say in my best Castilian, and he says he's honored to make my acquaintance, and then we're quiet.

Federico straightens with the Whitman in his hand. "Here you are."

"Thanks." But I don't move or start to leave.

Federico begins to look at me in that way he has, penetrating and curious, and Augusto stands. He stretches. "Think I'll take a little walk. Get some *aire fresca*," he says and tries to look casual.

Federico smiles at this. Decades, whole centuries, of European sophistication behind that smile, and I stand lost in his aristocratic aura.

Augusto goes out.

Forty-four

NOW IT'S REALLY AWKWARD.

I want to vanish, but Federico isn't disturbed, which helps a little.

He stands looking at me, trying to figure me out. I'm desperate—need to fill the air with talk—and then I remember. I dig in my pocket.

"I thought you'd want to see this."

I give him a clipping from *El Unico,* the Spanish weekly published in Miraflores. It's a report on the death of a Spaniard in a premature explosion and has to be the man Federico is grieving.

He takes the clipping, starts reading, and slowly lowers himself into his chair the way he did looking at the Freud when we first met, that evening still locked vivid in my mind. He takes his time, even rereads the article—it's short. Tears well in his eyes at one point but he doesn't seem to realize.

"May I have this?" he says and looks up at me.

"Of course."

"How do you see this paper? It's an anarchist publication. Surely your family doesn't read it."

"No. I buy it to practice my Spanish. And I like what it says."

He looks at me and I'm uncomfortable again, but I don't say anything. I let him study me.

"You are not a typical American."

I don't know how to answer that, but I consider it a compliment and say nothing. It makes me shy, the whole situation does, and I look away. He edges forward on his chair, leans his arms onto the table, and starts talking to me, urgently, quietly.

"This was the man, yes. Miguel Blanca y Ortez, a celebrated lawyer in Spain, like a father to me. He was fighting for the people." He lets that sink in. "Have you seen what it's like for the workers here, the labor camps? Lirio?"

"Yes, with Harry." But he hardly hears me.

"Tenements, that's all. Wobbly shanties with tin cans and washtubs and rickety chairs. It's the same everywhere—stairways breaking, small rooms, no windows. They hang cheap, dirty curtains to divide something they call the parlor from a five-foot bedroom for the whole family, and that's cluttered with junk and dirty blankets and breaking furniture . . ." I'm nodding and agreeing through all this. "Probably a prayer book under the baby in the basket, too. Old Voodoo worship—do you blame them? No chance for the children. They'll live the same way." He goes on, even more intense, his jaw muscles flexing, then finally he slows a little and looks straight at me.

"That's what we have in Spain—masses of peasants like that, living hopeless lives, nothing changing it." He leans even closer to make me understand. "It could change, you know. Everything could be different, but the Church hoards the money. Do you know about this?"

I want badly to say yes but I shake my head, an obedient good girl, honest. I do not know about peasant life in Spain.

"It's a terrible injustice, inexcusable, and Miguel was going to change it . . . under threat of death, always the threat of death. The Church doesn't like what he's doing. He's educated, a real danger to them, a writer, a lawyer, and he can get things done— *could* get things done. They have good reason to fear him, so they said cease or die. That was his choice, and we came here so he could stay alive, and now . . ."

He opens his arms in a gesture of despair, leans back exhausted, and in a plaintive voice says, "We were going back with money to raise a rebellion."

He goes completely quiet staring at the floor.

I have no idea what to say but I no longer want to disappear.

Forty-five

WHEN I FINALLY SPEAK, I HUMILIATE MYSELF.

"My father says Spaniards are the best workers—no trouble, hard working . . ."

He doesn't seem to notice how moronic that sounds.

"What does your father do?" he says.

"Railroads."

"Maybe I've seen him."

"Maybe."

"Or worked under him."

"Could be."

He looks at me. Again that penetrating stare, like seeing me for the first time. I hope it's as a viable human being, not just the American girl. The book girl, at least. I read *El Unico,* a wildly radical publication. I read good books. I have to be someone capable of understanding his ideals. I want him to see that. He looks at me with such intensity, I'm shaken, and again I want to bolt, but he starts talking. This time about conditions in Spain and the life of the peasants there, the injustice of the stranglehold the Church has on everything, and I realize that as I listen, the pieces I know about him are coming together. I see better what he's doing in this place, a man of uncommon intelligence working as a common laborer.

This whole thing, canal construction and the hard labor, is a theatrical backdrop for what really concerns him: the tragedy played out by his people, corrupt government, corrupt king, wretched corrupt Church. The canal's nothing, the labor only a means to an end.

The shacks in Lirio interest him, not the passage between the seas. It's what Harry talks about—the workers of the world, the all-powerful who run everything, the impoverished laborers making it possible. And in spite of my great marks in school and my interest in the larger picture, I know nothing about all this. Not in a firsthand visceral way. Federico may be aristocratic, but he knows the dirt and the toil better than I do by far.

He gestures, runs his hand through his hair, frustrated.

I still feel the heat hovering around my face and I hardly breathe.

I try to take in what he says and I do hear it, but what's going through my mind is something else. It's a picture of the two of us, a couple, in our house with Mother and Father.

There, the force field of rebellion coming off Federico doesn't fit, not in our quiet domestic scene.

My parents never talk about such things. Large world issues concerning the poor aren't in our lives. We give money to the church, to schools, to special funds for disasters, but there is no outrage or passion in the giving. We do our part only to help those in need, the regular business of decency.

We tithe but there's no emotion to it.

A bloodied body with parts hanging by strips of skin is unknown to us. That's a newspaper headline or a blurred photo—it's not something in our lives.

There's mildness in our giving, a sense of kindness and goodwill. Political fire is for the old world, Europe, and no closer than the pages of history books or the columns of the *Canal Record.*

Federico goes on about events in Spain, and I realize I know only what Mrs. Ewing presses on us in class, which sticks in me long enough for a high mark on a test, then it's gone.

The peasants of Spain aren't real, breathing human beings to me. Neither is the talk of war in Europe, though I've read about it. That's going to be thousands of miles away, fought between countries I'll never see by people I'm unlikely to meet. It will never involve Americans. I'm safe. I live on my Yankee island. I'm sequestered in my colonial Zone.

". . . we have to organize, force a change. It will take violence . . ." Federico's voice comes back and I make myself listen, come out of my dream, then he stops himself.

He looks me in the eye and the distance between us is gone. I'm not imagining this. He is no longer unapproachable.

He's human and I guess weakened by loss and grief, and I'm in the presence of that and, for a little while, inside it. My plan has worked better than I could have imagined. I'm right there with him and I'm softened into silence.

Forty-six

SUDDENLY HE SMILES. "The Whitman . . ." Just that fast, back on Earth.

I hold it up. "You gave it to me."

"Ah, right."

We're quiet. I feel small and dumb and silly again. Finally I say, "I have quite a bit to think about."

"Good," he says and stands. Our intense little encounter is over but something lingers—the closeness of his mentor's death. How do you wash blood out of a wooden floor? Or out of your life?

The usual pleasantries make no sense—we've gone too deep for that. No man—no human—has ever talked to me the way he has. Nobody's ever opened up to me like that.

I walk to the screened door and he follows and holds it open. It's inky dark outside.

"Isn't it dangerous out there for you?" he says.

"I'm a worker," I say, and my old kidlike ways come back. I pull the hat down over my face, stuff my hair into it, and give him a sly smile.

He looks me over. "I'm coming with you."

We walk along the track and I attempt to explain what a tomboy is, to justify my getup and willingness to pose as a worker at night. "It's an American expression," I say, thinking he doesn't know it.

"I've heard it in England," he says. "It's not considered bad or good, just a phase for certain young girls. But you are always ladylike at the Tivoli." Of course when I'm going to see him, I'm very much the lady.

We don't say much more, just pass a couple of workers carrying bottles in a hapless stagger. Then a woman passes with a bundle on her head and two children clutching her skirt, silent, never giving us a glance.

There's a heavy fragrance from the orchids hanging in the trees and clumps of orange flowers and amaryllis and wild lemon. I nearly trip on a vanilla vine. Federico reaches out and steadies me. I feel like a woman, not a kid helping Orville or Harry's androgynous pal. He steadies me and it's a natural movement between a man and a woman.

Neither of us speaks. When we get to my house he says good-bye and watches while I climb the steps. I go in the porch door and look back. He gives me a nod from below and a little smile and then he walks away.

It's still early and Mother asks where I've been.

"Sitting on the steps, sketching." Concern about lying is the last thing on my mind.

Forty-seven

WE'VE CROSSED A LINE. I'm now something more than Federico's supplier of books.

After the death of Miguel there's an understanding between us, but it's not the death that makes the change—it's talking about it with me.

I read *El Unico,* which he respects. I share his emotion for the loss of his mentor. I suggest new books from our library I know he'll want to read. But for me it's no longer about books. Federico has become pure desire.

True physical desire.

It cooks my dreams—daydreams at school, reveries on the

train, deep night dreams that wake me with their heat. This is the new world.

Still, I move carefully with plans for our meetings, proceeding with secrecy outside my parents' awareness. I make sure they think I'm at some school event or with friends or neighbors when we meet.

But we exchange books in open public places, never at his cabin, which is what I want. That would require some special arranging, and his thoughts, I'm fairly certain, are centered on his people, their rapacious government, and his anger at the Spanish Church—not on being alone with the American book-girl, no matter how much of a mind we are.

A new idea. I go to Mother.

"You know those events at the Ancon Women's Club?"

"Yes?"

"I think I'd like to attend a class."

"Oh, well . . ." She perks up, misperceives me completely, thinks I'm interested at last in homemaking skills.

She takes a list from a kitchen drawer that contains all the lectures the club has made available for Zoners. I sit down and study it, not the least bothered by how blatant and defiant my deception has become. It's a long list.

Native Fruits and How to Prepare Them.

Lace-Making and Mending.

A Lecture on Japan: Its People, Its Music, Its Art and Literature.

These are proper topics for intelligent conversation with which to snare a promising young man—I can see why Mother suddenly has hope.

The Women's Club in Las Cascadas is offering a dance class, Cristobal offers Shakespeare, and our own Culebra has announced a dramatization: the Battle of Lexington in colonial garb.

I study these—the meeting times, the content, the requirements —and the choice is simple: an art class. For my purposes it's just what I need.

Sketching: one hour.

Art appreciation: half an hour with comments by the instructor.

Break: twenty minutes, snack and tea.

Social hour: discussions of artwork.

That's the hour I'm focused on, that last one. I'll never have to return to the class after the break and I won't be missed, because I can see it's all going to be talk and chatter, looking at one another's sketches and gossiping. Technically I'll be in art class, my whereabouts accounted for, not expected at home until later, when the class is over.

That last hour is free. It will belong to me—and to Federico.

Forty-eight

THE PLAN GOES WELL. It becomes our regular meeting. Federico and I exchange books and talk after art class for more than an hour, but we're still formal. No more intense personal exchanges, not like the one about the death of Miguel. But we're much more at ease with each other. We discuss local labor issues, and he often mentions something he's heard from Spain. I quote *El Unico*. He quotes his fellow workers. But it's not personal, not intense.

I make sure I wear a fresh white dress, ironed before class. Mother smiles, pleased the class is having such a good effect on me. My shoes are clean and my hair brushed smooth. She's happy. So am I.

In the cool of the evening when we meet, Federico doesn't mention how I look, but he always gives me a quick once-over. It's unconscious, I think. He's always immaculate—his hair still damp from a shower, clean, simple workman's clothes. It's the best hour of my week, and I'm pretty much satisfied with the way it's going. Then, a month into the art-class meetings, it happens.

"Thanks for letting me keep these so long," he says.

"It's no problem." I give him two new volumes, he gives me the ones he's read.

I ask about Miguel, hoping to get more personal, always trying for that. "Is someone taking his place for you?"

"No, not really."

I can tell he wants to talk about it, so I'm direct. "Can you do what he was doing? Carry on for him?"

"I'm trying. We're a group, you know—there are many of us." He's walking me home at this point. "Movements are only as good as their leaders, and Miguel was the best." More walking.

Somebody laughs somewhere. A rooster crows for no reason on top of a hill. There's a sound of blasting in the distance.

"What is that?" I say.

"It's not in the Cut—it's the main channel through Gamboa."

"I've never seen it."

He looks at me again, more than just a glance. I meet his eyes but I don't know what it means.

"You should, you know. They're blasting trees." Still he looks at me.

"I want to see it," I say.

"Do you mean that?"

"Of course."

"Come on, then." He takes my hand and starts walking fast.

He leads me along the Cut, not a word, very fast, determined, holding my hand so I'll stay with him. The first time we've touched—something I expected to be electric but it's only practical. We pass other couples walking slowly, enjoying the balmy evening. We hurry a quarter mile up the Cut to the clearing crews.

I'm breathless when we get there, not a word exchanged the whole time. Then I can hardly believe my eyes.

Forty-nine

SPREAD BEFORE US ARE HUNDREDS OF TREE TRUNKS that remain after the cutting of the forest, an ugly stubble across the acreage. I've never seen it before. A blasting gang made up of West Indians is chopping holes into the stubby trunks, hacking with axes, moving fast, never looking up, sweat flying off their bodies. Federico still holds my hand in a protective grip, not affectionate. He walks me through the men, saying, "Look at this."

The workers hack away at a feverish pace and pay us no attention. As many as fifteen holes in a single trunk, put in two or three sticks of dynamite, add cap and fuse, then plaster it over with mud until all the holes are filled and they go on to the next trunk. We watch the furious work—hundreds of men surrounding us, hacking the trees and packing in dynamite, no talk, only hard labor.

Federico holds my hand with the grip of a parent. He's excited, his eyes shining, darting across the men and the dynamite sticks bristling from the trunks. We watch for a time, then a work whistle sounds and everything stops.

A pall drops over the whole area and the workers move off to the side. Federico squeezes my hand and pulls me away, forces me behind him, his glance still darting around the alien landscape.

In moments the laborers come back carrying lit torches in each hand. They stand at the farthest row of loaded trunks and wait. "We'll run with them," Federico says and squeezes my hand again.

I don't know what he means until it starts.

A whistle sounds and workers run back in among the trunks, and we run with them. Each worker lights his fuses, some trunks so large they have sixty-five or seventy dynamite sticks, and they run from one row to the next, from tree to tree, lighting fuses as fast as they can, the two of us with them at the edge of the wave of men moving across the stubbled forest, torches dipping and flying from trunk to trunk. Then behind us the first trunks begin to blow.

Chunks of trees fly into the air. Dirt rises and rains down. Red streaks the sky, and the men with us are still lighting the rows ahead.

The blasts creep forward in a wave from behind, my heart is bursting out of my chest. Federico never lets go of my hand—he pulls me along while the drum booms send spinning chunks of wood sky-high—thunderous, magnificent, one after the other. We reach the end gasping for breath and turn and watch the advancing explosions move across the blackened terrain—irregular, massive, huge clumps of wood lifting into the sky, branches and dirt and more blasts, and then the last explosions and quiet. The air clears and the workers move back in—they aren't finished. They do this every night.

Federico leads me to a grassy hill off to the side. He lets go of my hand and we sit and watch. The laborers gather the splintered wood and pile it into gigantic heaps. They douse the heaps with crude oil, waves of the acrid scent drift to us, then one by one they touch off the stacks and the bonfires flare, looping high into the sky with crackling, breaking sounds. Federico never once looks away. The hell roars boom in front of us. The closer fires snap and pop as they eat through the remaining wood.

What I know of blasting is in the Cut where Father does his work, and it's mild compared to this—battalions of tripod and Star drills run by compressed air pounding and grinding and jamming holes into the rock, followed by gangs of powder men, always black, of course, with boxes of dynamite that they carelessly throw down and then pound the drill holes full of explosives. They blow at 11:30, when the men are at lunch, and at 5:30, when they've gone home—mighty explosions, twice a day in addition to the ongoing smaller ones that make our porch chairs rock and Mother's cakes fall and are heard out at sea.

But this, the clearing of the woods, I've never seen, only heard about vaguely. It's not a difficult part of the dig and Father has never mentioned it. To me it's staggering. And I don't know why Federico has me sitting with him to watch it.

Fifty

THE BONFIRES FINALLY DIE DOWN and still Federico stares at them. He's transported and pensive, somewhere else. Finally he takes a deep breath and turns to me.

"What do you think?" A quaver in his voice.

I shake my head, amazed, still breathless from running and the exhilaration of what I've seen. I smile, go serious, smile again, and shake my head in confusion. I don't know what he wants from me. "It's incredible," I say.

He looks out over the scattered glowing embers and says, "I love it."

"Why?"

"It reminds me of home."

I go quiet again and look at the blackened landscape. Can't quite imagine what he means. There's an occasional pop or breaking sound. The workers move along the periphery, black silhouettes striking at flaring spots along the edges and speaking to one another as workers do during the most common workday.

Federico stands.

He holds his hand out to me, not like a parent this time.

I reach for him. His grip is soft and he keeps his eyes on my face.

We start walking but not in a rush. He holds my hand gently. It makes me forget what we've just seen. I'm seventeen. Still in school. I'm on another planet.

We pass other couples and workers along the way. When we're at the meadow in front of the Tivoli, he stops and we look back at the glow of diminishing fires.

"It's beautiful," I say.

He moves me against him and holds me. I feel him, his sex, between us and I don't pull away. He holds me a long while—it seems very long—and I embrace him, embarrassed at the pounding of my heart that he must feel, embarrassed at not being more sophisticated.

To the side is the gazebo belonging to the Tivoli but overgrown in disuse. The sagging structure stands a few yards off the path, almost hidden by weeds and completely abandoned. He leads us inside, pulls me to him again, and presses us together.

He begins to reach in my clothes and I help, unbutton and unhook and he pulls me against him over and over. His breathing gets heavy and he lays me down and caresses me and makes love to me, trying to be gentle but needing it so much that toward the end he pleads softly, "Hold me . . . hold me."

I'm overwhelmed and my emotion is so powerful, I don't feel any discomfort of my own—there must be some. I'm only holding him and feeling how much he needs me. *He needs me.* Then I lie quiet in his arms and he shudders a last time, still holding me against him.

I can't think of anything to say until I'm aware of the warm streak between us and think there might be some correct behavior about that.

Finally he lifts himself and says, "Are you all right?"

"Yes . . ." I take a stab at the right thing: "Are you?"

A soft laugh comes out of him. "Yes." He wipes his shirt across my belly.

"I know . . . I know what to do," I say. A desperate attempt at sexual savvy.

"You do?" He doesn't believe me.

"Yes, don't worry." But I don't know what to do or how to behave—I don't know anything.

We put our clothes back on and pull the weeds and grass from each other's hair and clothing—sexual camaraderie, like old friends. We stand and he runs his hands down my arms.

"I'm all right," I say.

We make our way through the vines that cover the gazebo and walk slowly along the track until we're at the steps to my house. He seems disturbed and says, "You have to be careful."

"I will be."

He leans in and gives me a kiss on the cheek and embraces me again. He needs to say something—I see him searching.

"Bring me books tomorrow?" is what he finally says.

Books. "Of course," I say, trying to sound like nothing is different and I don't come from a sheltered life and I'm not naive or in an outrageously heightened state.

I go up the steps, affect a business-as-usual manner, and from inside the porch look down at him through the screen door. I raise my hand and he gives me a little nod, then turns and walks away.

It *Is* a New World
Fifty-one

I SIT WITH MAMIE LEE KELLY, the best known of all Americans on the Isthmus. The local madam. And I've done my homework. My diary is full of thoughtful entries on my new life—what I have to do, have to learn, how to proceed.

Miss Kelly comes from New Orleans and runs the Navajo, a brothel on I Street in Panama City. She's lusty, large, and voluptuous, and she appears to be very capable. This makes me confident.

"Hell yes, honey, I can tell you a whole shitload of things to do," she says. She leans back on her red velvet settee and draws hard on a cigarette. She cocks her head to one side, grins, and looks me over. "Got yourself a young man?"

"Yes. And there's no talking to my mother . . ."

"Course not. Not her business." Mamie grins widely again. "Mothers don't know everything and they usually know the least about what they should know the most." I'm not exactly sure what she means. "Sex!" she says and laughs.

Sex can be dangerous—I know that. A foolish mistake will always be with me, can shame and destroy Mother and Father.

There's no need for that. Mamie can get it all under control. She goes dead serious.

"How old are you, again?" she says.

"Seventeen."

"Mmm." She looks me over carefully. "You've done it with him?"

"Yes. Once. I'm not pregnant."

"Good, you're lucky. And smart—you're here. Good girl. Sorry you can't work for me." Another big laugh. I take the suggestion as a compliment. A couple of her "girls" sidle by in tatty chenille dressing gowns, pasty faces, and stringy hair, but it's early for them at eleven in the morning. They're just getting up. Others walk by in the hall with cups of coffee and what look like corn-bread muffins. They glance in and dismiss me with surly looks.

The place is strange and I lied an hour earlier to get here. Told Mrs. Ewing I felt sick and she sent me home. I'll need another lie tomorrow to get back in class, but it will be only a half lie—my time of the month and discomfort, et cetera. Perfect. A love affair is no simple matter and it isn't all romance.

"I'll tell you something, sweetheart," Mamie says. "There's an old method just right for you. Dates, acacia, a little honey—grind them together, dip it in cotton wool, and put it right in there. Acacia ferments, becomes lactic acid—that's a worldwide spermicide." The laugh again. "Just right for a worldwide young man . . . where's he from?"

"Spain," I say, and I don't smile. "I suspect sperm are the same everywhere."

Her face goes straight and she says, "I really am sorry you can't work for me."

Fifty-two

THERE IS EVERYTHING IN PANAMA AMONG THE LOCALS. Making my way through the vendors outside the Navajo, I find acacia quick enough. I know I won't find it at the commissary. Honey and dates Mother has at home—she makes wonderful date bread. The acacia is cheap and there's plenty.

Later in the evening, alone in the kitchen with Mother's mortar and pestle, I blend my little concoction and wonder how long it will be good. If fermentation is so important, maybe age is a good thing, and I regret not asking Mamie about that. But I conclude that if it's such a crucial matter she would have told me. I can make small amounts as needed. I'm ready.

But I don't hear from Federico for several days.

Up to now that hasn't been unusual, but after what happened in the gazebo, I don't know what to think. He isn't there after the art class either. I wait in the darkness outside a long time, then go back inside and chat. (*What era was Poussin? And what were the politics? I love the way you're doing your hair.*) I have to escape.

He isn't at the Tivoli when I pass there on Sunday with Mother and Father.

He isn't at any of our regular meeting places, which baffles me, and I toughen myself for the worst. I resolve not to be a whimpering sissy. I can barely make myself imagine what this could mean.

More days go by.

He's dropped out of sight. I can't sleep. At school I can't concentrate or work. I have to do something.

It's one more time along the track at night after another "sketching on the steps" excuse for Mother—slouched hat and jodhpurs.

I climb the stairs to his cabin. I feel nervous and out of place, much worse than the first time I went there. Everything seems so complicated. I never imagined how sex could complicate things. At the door I can see his cot. It's empty—only Augusto is there.

"Augusto . . ." He looks up, surprised. *"Federico no está . . . ?"*

"Al hospital," he says and lets me in.

"Hospital?"

He explains. Ancon Hospital, ward 30. It's serious. I sink onto a chair.

Frederico got feverish while he was working, Augusto tells me, and couldn't swing his pick. The doctor came, examined him, and wanted to know if he believed in God, because he was going to die.

"Why would a doctor say a thing like that?"

Augusto doesn't know, but the doc wrote up the papers and put him on the train to the hospital. In the ward he was so weak with fever, the nurses had to hold him up. They gave him an ice bath and he told Augusto he thought he really would die.

"You've seen him?" I say.

"The next day. They were making him drink quinine every two hours." A vile, bitter liquid—I shudder for him.

"Could I see him, do you think?"

Augusto doesn't think so.

Fifty-three

"No, no visitors."

"I'm a relative."

"No. No one goes in the typhoid ward." That's where he's been moved.

The nurses' station is busy, and the women in white are moving fast. There's very little casual conversation—everybody's courteous but preoccupied.

"Isn't there anything I can do?" I'm pleading with the nurse, hoping she'll see something in my eyes—fear for his life, desperation, something.

She's sympathetic and says for me to leave a note and she'll make sure he gets it. I'm grateful for that and she gives me paper. "Thank you, thank you."

I crush the first note and write another. I crumple it, too, remembering a nurse will have to read it to him, can't be too personal. The next note says something about finding out from Augusto the night before, he shouldn't give up hope and it begins to sound like I'm saying he's at death's door.

I tear that one up and write another. I take my time. I'm more positive, talk about getting well, efficient nurses, skilled doctors, advanced medicines, he'll be out in no time. It sounds good.

"I'll take it to him right away," says the nurse, and she puts it in her pocket and moves on with her tray. This is a busy place. Federico might die.

He Doesn't

Fifty-four

"I WAS SO DELIRIOUS WITH FEVER AND WEAK from not eating that it wasn't read to me for days," Federico says. We're walking in the hills, only a few people wandering by. "I was dying and I wasn't afraid."

His first day out of the hospital and he's with me. Who else does he have? Augusto working, Miguel dead, I'm the one. His near-death sickness is over, he's getting well, and we're a couple. It's been a nightmare for me. Worse for him.

I'm in my best white dress with a parasol because I know he likes it. It's clear to anyone who sees us that I'm his woman, because we're walking together, a form of courting in the Zone.

But we're not consciously courting—at least, he's not. He needs to talk about what's happened—the weeks of awful illness, the hospital treatments, how he felt the whole time—and I'm the one to hear it. I've never been so elated. Peaceful, too, though I've lied to Mother. She thinks I'm helping Mrs. Ewing.

"It's not a bad thing to know about yourself—that you're not afraid of dying," he says. "I had terrible dreams. Black ugly shapes and voices—I don't know what they were saying, but talking loud and swarming at me, and all I wanted was to go to sleep. I wanted death, back to before I was born, just to get out of the nightmare."

We walk slowly, the backs of our hands brushing from time to time, no other contact. "Then, after days of that—I don't know how long—I heard the night nurse talking to me, could barely hear her voice. And I came out of it a little, and she helped me drink some milk, the first thing I'd had in days, then I went back to sleep. But there were no dreams anymore, and I began to drink milk every day and I started wanting to live because the nurse kept talking to me and her voice was kind. She made it sound like it mattered to her—my living . . ."

"It matters to me," I say.

"I know." He smiles. "That's when the nurse asked if I wanted to hear the note you dropped off. She asked if it was from my girl."

"And you said . . ."

"Yes." He doesn't look me in the eye, just smiles.

We pass a tourist couple in colorful clothes. They look German. Probably weekly arrivals, in on the Hamburg-American Line.

They watch us pass, and I know we are a handsome couple. Federico doesn't notice, though. "Everything smells good again," he says and breathes deep.

It's dry season, hot but not insufferable. The air is heavy with the scent of exotic flowers and local food.

The women we pass glance at Federico, a handsome man who looks better than the others in spite of being pale and thin from his ordeal. Or maybe because of it.

I puff with pride. I wish we could hold hands, but it would be too daring, a worker and an American girl, though no one would guess he's on the labor force. Instinctively we observe the rules of our dangerous liaison.

"Then what?" I say.

"They put me on a regular diet and gave me pajamas."

"You had no pajamas?"

"Only a hospital gown. Pajamas meant I could get out of bed and move around. But I could barely walk. I needed a nurse on each side to hold me up. I walked every day and ate. I ate a lot—porridge, eggs, bread, melon. I was getting well . . ." I nod and smile, completely content.

Fifty-five

HE'S WEARING A BEAUTIFULLY TAILORED WHITE SUIT.

"Where did it come from?" I ask.

"A doctor. A reader like you. I promised to loan him several books, some from you. We have the same favorite philosophers, and this doctor, American, said it was rare to find really informed readers among the Zoners. Of course he was surprised to talk with me, a worker. We had long conversations. It made the time pass."

"Books, huh?"

We exchange an intimate smile.

He tells me the doctor is a "devoted Hegelian." "Imagine discussing dialectic in this morass of—" Federico stops himself. "I won't complain. I'm happy to be alive and he gave me the suit. He's put on weight and can't wear it."

The suit is a very fine light wool. "Absolutely cool in the heat and the fit is nearly perfect, except for the length of the pant legs. He arranged for the alterations."

Through the streets of Ancon we walk. I listen to his story, love being close to him, take pride in the looks we get, both of us in our best white garments. Quick nods from passing businessmen, jealous looks from two young women on their way to the commissary, obsequious nods from vendors. We appear to be tourists. Then, at one of the vendors' carts, the truth bites us.

"*Dos,*" Federico says and pays for the guava drinks with silver coins. And there it is: he's a silver-roll employee. Only Americans are paid on the gold roll. Everyone else is silver—two lines on payday.

The vendor looks perplexed, a worker, not working, in such a fine suit? But the vendor goes back to his cart and we continue walking. I dismiss the little event. No one else knows the color of coins in Federico's pockets.

We pass Mamie and get a double glance. She gives me an approving smile, then moves along. I pretend I don't see her.

Finally, back in his cabin, Federico slumps on his cot and breathes hard. I can see how weak he is. He's trembling.

"You should rest," I say.

He looks at me suddenly and sees my worry. "Can you come back tomorrow?"

"Of course. What do you need?"

"Nothing . . . you."

A walloping flop in my chest. "All right," I say.

He pulls me to him and gives me a chaste kiss. I'm afraid he'll feel my heart going and know that I'm shaking because I'm still not sophisticated about any of this, especially this day of reunion and secretive walking and not really knowing who we are together.

He must perceive all that because he gives me a smile as he watches me leave, and for that I'm grateful.

Outside the cabin, walking along the track, I make the quick assumption we're still a couple, lovers after all these weeks. I'm important to him. The books are important, but I am too now.

I'm soon walking on air—that's exactly how it feels, and those sappy expressions that always made me roll my eyes, they're right on the money. Who's the fool now? And the long, enthusiastic entry in my diary that night sounds like a fool's babble. That's fine with me.

Fifty-six

NEXT DAY IN HIS CABIN: "She runs a brothel and knows about these things," I say to Federico. "I trust her."

He's smiling, almost laughing, and pulls me against him. "You really aren't like anybody," he says—that perplexed/amazed look again.

"I'm a tomboy."

"But I don't see that in you. There's no boy in there . . ." He begins peeling off my clothes piece by piece, smiling, looking at me, enjoying the looking especially when I'm stripped down to nothing. He pulls off his own clothes and I see how thin the sickness made him. He lays me on his cot, then puts himself beside me and presses my back to his chest. He tucks his knees behind mine and we're quiet together, his hand on my belly just grazing the bristle between my legs, his sex neatly fitted against my backside.

It's midafternoon, still two hours until the work whistle goes and another forty-five minutes after that until Augusto arrives. We have plenty of time. As for Mother, she thinks I'm still at school doing special-assignment work. And the work camp where we are—nobody is around; it's empty. We're alone in limbo.

He holds me quietly, breathing softly. A jungle bird squawks somewhere and dogs bark. A double explosion goes off in the Cut. He begins to caress me, his strong grip gradually pressing me to him.

We make love in a different way, not with the desperation I felt from him in the gazebo, but slowly, something luxurious that takes a long time.

I am an apt pupil and have no sense of time or place, no sense of the heat except our own, and I'm lost in sensuality. I follow his lead—I'm willing, focused, totally without self-consciousness, and I can't imagine we'll stop, ever, my sexual fever so roused, my brain so numb. Our sexual play goes on a long time, or it seems to, judging by my limited experience, and then it does end as it should and I find I like the viscous warmth he's pooled on my belly in spite of what I've told him about Mamie, and I rub my hand in it and across my breasts—a slick, wonderful feel. He watches me do that with a look of pleasure and slight amazement, and we are finished. I've pleased him, and he has most certainly pleased me, which wasn't hard to do—I can see he likes that. I'm good at this.

I feel my body settle and we lie quiet, like dolls in a box, on that tiny cot, drifting, half dozing, with no thoughts—none for me, anyway.

In time we begin to talk about my parents.

"They have no idea," I say.

"What if they find out?"

"They can't. They cannot."

It's a serious matter—we know it.

We watch two beetles wobbling along the windowsill beside us. It makes us laugh—sexual camaraderie again. Everything is all right.

GOING STEADY

Fifty-seven

THE NEXT WEEKS OF HIS RECOVERY we spend in long erotic afternoons. I learn a lot and he's happy.

After sex we talk about how isolated we both feel; he's literally distant from the people he knows and cares about, and I feel remote from my parents even though I see them every day. He won't talk about his family, but he tells me about friends in Madrid.

"We sit in cafés and rail against Spanish politics and the Church and the whole mess . . . We're on fire, all of us. Our little band is not so little anymore from what I hear, and it will be even bigger when I go back."

It sounds important and worldly and weighty to me. "Our neighbors, the Wrights, they're my little band, I guess, but they're not remotely rebellious. Wil and Orville Wright, the fliers—you know them?"

"The brothers Wright?"

"Next-door neighbors, my best friends." Frederico raises his head and looks at me with frowning disbelief, and I realize that without trying I've impressed him at least as much as his country's miserable Church has impressed me. "I grew up hanging out with them, not with my school friends or my parents. I can't talk to my parents at all."

He's still on the boys. "The Wrights?" He can't believe it.

"They lived next door is all."

"Amazing." He laughs and gives my chin a jiggle. "Listen, you're not supposed to be able to talk to your parents. Every generation is different. We have to find parents in the life we lead."

"Is Miguel the father you found?" I can say this kind of thing to him now—sex does that.

"I guess he is—was."

A moment passes and I say, "How did it happen?" He knows I mean the explosion that killed Miguel.

He sits up and braces his arm across me. We're both shiny with sweat from sex and dry-season heat.

"We were leaving for the noon meal—fifty-two holes loaded, charges tamped in, fuses set, everything ready. Nothing was different that I remember, just another day. The last holes went down fifty feet through solid rock for two hundred yards along the Cut, but there was nothing different about that. It's a big blast to set but we do it all the time. It was supposed to go off while we were at lunch, and then, when we were still climbing out . . ."

"What did you do?"

"Started digging soon as the blast settled. I knew where he was—the lowest channel. Had to be tons of rock on him. We got a few men out alive, the ones near the surface, but Miguel . . ." He takes a moment remembering, seeing it again. "He was almost decapitated."

He lies back and pulls me on top of him. I sprawl there, his arms holding me, thinking he'll tell me more, but he doesn't. I feel him slowly relaxing, and after a while he sighs and I close my eyes and we both doze off.

When we wake a little later there's no more talk about Miguel or Spain. Only about sex—my fine legs, which he says should be noticed for as long as I live. *Typical of tomboys, are they?* he says. *No? Just your own gift, then?* More stroking, a mention of our fine fit, more sex involving the innocent hammock, and then it's time for Augusto to return. I wash and dress and sit on Frederico's lap.

"Do you dream about me?" I ask. Even if he doesn't, I want him to say he does.

"Of course."

I choose to believe him.

After that I go home and we never talk about Miguel again, or dreams, or need to.

In my diary that night I record the whole afternoon—the sex, the conversation, everything I can remember—in vivid detail, going on and on for pages, then add, *All this is passing way too fast. Can't let myself think about that.*

It's an afterthought from nowhere and it's disturbing.

Fifty-eight

I'M GETTING REALLY GOOD AT LYING. That's because it gets a lot of deliberation. I plan things at night before I go to sleep, and I've developed a system that works because it's executed perfectly.

After all, the payoff for success in seeing Federico is huge and the penalty for getting caught is catastrophic, so I can't and I don't make errors. I am thoughtful with my parents, think carefully before I speak without fail, and always cover my tracks.

To begin with, I lard the whopper of the day with a sliver of truth. It puts me at ease, and the look I give Mother is clear-eyed—I've learned to do that. Some of my excuses to leave school early and arrive home late in order to extend the afternoons with Federico are true, they just don't take as long as I lead her to believe. And all the excuses are logical—that goes without saying. I don't allow any pattern to develop that might rouse her suspicion. I keep the excuses listed in a notebook, which I lock away, tick each one off as I use it, keeping them in random order. No pattern—that's important. It goes something like this:

1. Long hours in the library
2. Working on a report
3. Studying for a test (with a friend or on my own, rotated)
4. Working with another student on a project (at the friend's house)
5. Working on a project on my own (at school)
6. Helping Mrs. Ewing (always true)

And there are more, all of them based on simple Midwestern horse sense. How can I go wrong?

My marks on tests and reports are higher than ever and Mother doesn't question me. Still, I give her my schedule every morning whether she asks for it or not, further confirming my dependability—*what a remarkable girl*—while other teens are running wild. She's grateful for my obedience but doesn't say so—it's no more than she expects.

My grades buy an enormous amount of freedom, and I see no harm in using it any way I want; I don't even see harm in the deception. I'm breaking away from my family gently, without mutinous rebellion. One day they'll be grateful for this. If they ever know about it.

Fifty-nine

THE DAYS GO BY, EACH ONE IN THE FOLLOWING ORDER. I arrive at Federico's cabin after school. By then he's completed his exercises. He's disciplined and never fails to go through the program he created for himself to rebuild his strength. He lifts logs, climbs a hanging vine several times, pushes a tree trunk up his hill over and over like Sisyphus, takes long hikes. I admire his ability to do this. I think I have the same discipline but have never had the chance to test it. And he reads.

There are designated hours for these exercises of his. They start at first light, about four thirty. He and Augusto get up with the work whistle. Augusto goes down the hill to catch the work train; Federico goes up the hill to his climbing vine. The drill begins. He does some basic exercises to loosen his muscles (he's explained all this to me seriously), then climbs the vine. He goes through the whole routine, rests, regains his strength, then starts again. This goes on until eleven when he eats with the other workers. The doctor recommended he get on the workers' diet as soon as possible—his body needs to accustom to the rigors of pick and shovel. So he waits by the track and hops on the labor train when it comes by, headed for the mess hall.

This train has two enclosed "gold" coaches for Americans and open cattle cars with long benches for the sweating "silver roll" workmen. Six hundred of them jam onto flatcars, riding in the sun to the mess halls. Let there be no mistake: Americans are kept as comfortable as possible. Workers of color are simply processed with the greatest possible efficiency. I've become acutely aware of this, thanks to Harry.

The wooden mess-hall tables are stocked with rough food, the kind needed for prolonged physical labor, and Federico eats with his Spanish buddies and enjoys their company. All this is part of his regimen; he judges his recovery by how much he needs to consume. When he eats as much as he did before the sickness, he'll know he is expending the same amount of energy in his exercises as he uses for work. He will never quite burn the energy of *pico y pala*, but he's rebuilding his muscles, and eating with his Spanish friends is stoking his political fire.

"We talk politics," he tells me, "and I get news about the king and the atrocities . . ." He shakes his head. "They never end." His eyes flash; the insurrectionist in him kindles. I can see him in the streets, leading the workers, urging solidarity. It excites me. Always.

After lunch Federico goes outside the mess hall, lies in the grass, and dozes until the screech of the labor whistle. Exertion, food, rest—he is building back daily.

When the train comes by, he rides to his cabin, where he showers and reads and waits. I arrive an hour later.

The Best of Times
Sixty

This is our honeymoon.

Neither of us has any particular responsibilities. Our daily rendezvous is the center of our lives. The time is limited, a few weeks at most, having whole afternoons together instead of secret evenings, and we make the most of it. I have access to everything, so I bring treats from the cold storage plant at Cristobal.

I make every day a party: ice cream and frozen puddings and the local juices in bottles still so cold they have a jacket of fog in the sultry heat. French delicacies from the bakery, millefeuilles and buttery croissants, and elegant tarts and cakes with extravagant decorations, and sometimes little meat pies and chef's concoctions that bewilder us as to their content but are always delicious. And every time I remember to bring something for Augusto.

"Para Usted," I say to him.

"Gracias," he says, and has to smile.

One time, Federico and I lie naked together when Augusto comes back from work. This is after nearly two weeks, and we don't move as we hear him coming up the steps. He's dripping with sweat after twelve hours in punishing heat, and when he walks in he jerks to a stop. Federico has flung the edge of a sheet across me but not himself—we're lovers in bed in the late afternoon. (It's about four thirty. Mother's cooking supper, thinks I'm building a diorama at school. Father's just finished redirecting tons of volcanic rock onto flatcars.)

"Flagrante delicto," Federico says to Augusto, laughing, and waves an arm at a plate on the table. *"Tu piña helado."*

"Lazy brute," Augusto says. He takes the melting ice cream, grins, and goes out to the front step to eat.

We go to the makeshift shower—our ritual—and soap and rinse and dry each other. I put on my school clothes and hang my canvas bookbag over my shoulder.

Flagrante delicto rings in my head and I wonder. "You studied law?"

"Something like that." His soft smile means "enough."

I don't press it.

My senses are so electrified by these afternoons, it's hard to stop touching him. We kiss, kiss again, and finally I go out the front door. When I pass Augusto—he's finished the last of the *helado*—he thanks me in English.

"De nada," I say, but I don't like the sound of the word *nada.* It's true bringing him ice cream is nothing at all, but the afternoons are far from nothing and they're about to end. They are the biggest thing in my life, but Federico is getting stronger and nearly ready for work and this interlude is almost over. *"De nada"* won't pass my lips again.

A few days later Federico says it: "I'm fit for labor." He uses the sardonic tone he saves for comments about the Spanish king.

"My weight is normal, muscles strong—the doctor says I can go back to work."

To this "good" news, neither of us smiles.

Sixty-one

THE LAST AFTERNOON TOGETHER WE'RE IN THE HILLS above the Cut where long grass billows in the breeze. Father and Mother won't be anywhere near. We're safe.

Federico is troubled and I know why. His self-esteem is back after being away from the Cut and not subjected to humiliating remarks from American workers because he's a digger. Now he has to return to sneers from shovel engineers and numbing labor in the infernal heat. It's got to be hard for him. I have to think he's lectured himself that it's right to endure what the peasants endure so he can serve them better, some magnanimous thing like that, which doesn't help when you feel worthless. And he won't indulge his feelings and complain to me—that would negate the whole thing.

He could talk to Harry about this. He'd understand completely and agree. They could be great friends, these two men in my life—common ideals, common values.

Then Federico speaks and it's as though he's heard my thoughts. "They put themselves at a great height, you know, feeling superior because they earn more."

"Exactly," I say.

"I suppose they need to feel better about themselves."

"Crane man Ned, Harry's old roommate, thinks he's quite a card and very superior, and he's a drunk. I know it for a fact."

"Yes?"

"Hangs out with the Panamanians at their jungle stills. Harry says he's a bully, too. Harry roomed with him till he couldn't stand it anymore."

"Harry's a good man."

"Yes." I can't resist. "Once Harry was talking about enumerating and he said, 'Do you remember that fellow Federico? The one we came across who has books and a neat cabin?'"

A rare grin breaks on Federico's face. "And you said?"

"I said yes."

"That's all?"

"What else could I say? He was talking about the various interesting people he meets, that kind of thing . . ."

Frederico pulls me to him and hugs me to his side as we walk. At that moment I am his closest friend.

The hills are burnished yellow by the sun, and people are walking all around us, sightseeing. He begins talking about his friends in Spain and how much he misses them. Hugged against him I know we are close, but I feel him begin to slip away as always, off to the place he'd rather be.

"We walk along the Paseo de Recoletas in Madrid every evening," he says. "Everyone comes out. We eat later there, not before eight, then we go out walking and meet and talk." Nothing Dayton-like about that. "They take away the public benches by nine so you pay a little something to sit in a chair—they're stacked away during the day. And there's a band that comes in later and plays—local musicians, a couple of blind violinists are usually with them. And we buy a paper and talk about politics. *El País, El Heraldo, La Correspondencia*—they all have different points of view. Everybody has an opinion . . ." I hear the pleasure in his voice. His eyes are lit. I'm nowhere in this memory, pressed against his side but distant. "And the music doesn't end until three, sometimes later, and even then it might still be too hot to sleep . . ."

I try to picture it, a world millions of miles from anything I know and Federico with his friends, not with me. It pains me and, trying to enter that world, I say, "Tell me about the Prado. I've never been there or any museum with paintings of the masters."

"Ah, too crowded," he says, still only faintly aware of me. I've relocated his memory only a few Madrid blocks, not back to us. "I went there as a boy and sketched everything—Pre-Raphaelites to Goya. I'd spend whole days there. I brought food in a little bag and sketched and copied. I was as serious as a master, imagined myself apprentice to the greats . . ." His smile fades. "But . . . other things took over and . . ."

I did sketching like that with Michelangelo's drawings, but not in a museum. From a book. I don't mention this puny artistic effort of mine.

He finally looks at me seriously, as though I might be going to the Prado tomorrow, and says, "The paintings are hung too close—you can't see one for the other."

"I'll remember that."

He misses my irony and goes on seriously. "You'll see great works someday," he says. "In New York maybe, when you go home."

And that takes my breath away.

Sixty-two

AT THAT FIRST MENTION OF SEPARATION we crest a grassy hill and come on a guided tour of mostly Europeans; they're coming now by the thousands. I put my mind on them, try to escape the thought of leaving. I imagine the once-in-a-lifetime opportunity this afternoon is for them. Photos taken that day will be handed down for generations with stories to tell the children and grandchildren: "We saw the oceans being connected." History in family snapshots.

The men wear white shoes and straw hats; the ladies are in white ankle-length dresses with parasols. I wonder if styles will really change much in the future and how and if they will be better, more functional. I doubt it. The tourists wear the uniform of the Zone—colonialists in white—and they look out over the Cut, awed as the guide pitches his voice for them to hear:

"You are now overlooking the special wonder of the canal, the world-famous Culebra Cut, nine miles between Bas Obispo and Pedro Miguel. Nothing else matters if the stretch you see here cannot be accomplished." Federico listens with a stern look.

"It is the first man-made canyon in history, and that swarming mass of laborers you see down there and the trains and shovels are breaking the spine of the Cordilleras, the Continental Divide." The people gaze below, enthralled. "There is more tonnage per mile moving on those tracks than on any railroad in the world, and I assure you, folks, the noise and heat are merciless." The guide lets that sink in, then says, "Enjoy the breeze!" And the group laughs and moves on.

We stand still. "I'll be there tomorrow," Federico says.

Spain and his friends and the Madrid evening are gone. I am all that's left.

He's still elegant in his white suit—very European, every inch an aristocrat and himself again after weeks of recovering, making love, talking about politics and life. But I'm not really a part of it. I'm still outside looking in.

He looks down at the famous inferno below us.

"Tomorrow . . ." he says, and he's not happy.

Sixty-three

WE GO BACK TO HIS CABIN, both aware of the finality of our *honeymoon* but not mentioning it. We lie on his cot fully clothed and don't make love. We listen to the parrots, the rumble of work in the Cut, a conversation in Portuguese down the hill, a couple of people arguing. I know Federico has drifted away. He is thoughtful, probably still in Madrid with Spanish friends, certainly not with me.

When I have to leave, he walks with me back toward our house, holding my hand, absent. I don't try to talk to him. Better leave him alone when he's like this. I'm the good, obedient girl.

When it is no longer safe for us to be seen together, he says goodbye. We don't make plans to meet again and he goes back along the track toward his cabin, hardly noticing anything around him. I continue on alone.

An unsettling afternoon. I don't know what comes next.

Sixty-four

CATASTROPHE, THAT'S WHAT.

I'm not a catastrophist and I'm not exaggerating. It's the biggest slide of the entire dig. A massive movement of earth in a section of canal called Cucaracha, a problem spot for years. It breaks loose again that night.

Next morning when Federico shows up with the other workers, they find some steam shovels buried in mud to the tips of their cranes, others entirely covered. It's not a complete surprise.

"It's been threatening for weeks," Father said, mentioning the danger one evening over pork roast and fried apples. "A lot of instability in Cucaracha."

And when it happens, it takes down nearly fifty acres from the canal's edge, a tropical glacier. Five hundred thousand cubic yards of mud straight into the Cut, across the floor, and to the other side. Hundreds of miles of track disappeared or twisted into crazed patterns. One shovel and a stretch of track picked up and deposited unharmed halfway across the floor. No other slide has done anything like it.

I see the disaster from the train on my way to school and wonder where Federico is in this mess. I know he's safe—the slide was at night—but he has to be shoveling the sucking sludge with hundreds of others and no longer in his white suit. It's all wrong. And it's all I can see while we talk about the slide in class—him working like a peasant in the Cut and of course flashes of sex, the two of us on the hammock or on the cot or against the cabin wall.

"Such slides are inevitable," says Mrs. Ewing. "The engineers are ready with dredges and there will be more slides, no doubt about it, but the canal will be built anyway. Don't worry about that."

I don't.

When I get home I expect to hear about a delay or even a complete rethinking of the work—months of digging have been deposited back into the canal and it seems to me like a defiant stroke of nature, something for them to consider in future work. I wonder what Father will say about it.

"Hell, we'll dig it out again." He isn't bothered. He's home at the regular time and is especially buoyed, taking a second helping of glazed carrots, quoting Colonel Goethals: "Go back to work, boys."

Mother frowns at the use of "hell" at the table. Father doesn't notice—he admires Goethals's confidence too much to let her dampen his spirits.

". . . he went off in that yellow railcar and everybody started digging again—those strong boys just went right back to work. We saved what we could of the rails and dug out an engine. Thank heaven it happened at night—nobody injured. Pass the gravy, please. We're rebuilding the tracks and digging up the twisted rails—got to haul those away . . ."

"What if the slides continue," I say, "get so frequent the canal's never completed and letting in ocean water would only make a muddy gully?" Father looks at me, amazed, a silent half smile, half frown at my crazy notion.

I pursue it. "It looks like that's the direction it's going and nature's choosing it. Couldn't that happen?"

"No, no, no, could never happen . . ." he says, that unstoppable attitude again. "Mr. Roosevelt has been here," he reminds me, as though that's the answer. And he says no more.

Mr. Roosevelt is not God. He is not even in office now. He certainly cannot shore up the canal walls. But he was here, all right, all eyeglasses and flashing teeth. Struck a nice pose sitting in a white suit and hat at the controls of a giant Bucyrus shovel in rain that dogged his entire visit, and the photographs filled local papers and newspapers in the States for weeks with descriptions of the president's can-do attitude in spite of the downpour.

I won't argue Roosevelt and confidence with Father. His attitude is admirable and not unlike the Wrights, who just went on and on to success. They did fly. A month before they flew, the *New York Times* said it would take a million years for man to fly—the boys pointed it out to me, amused. Then a few weeks later, on my birthday, they flew, fifty-nine seconds of heavier-than-air flight a million years too early. So much for projections. I don't want to be the *New York Times* in this situation. Too many deaths so far, too much effort, too much genuine travail for my naysaying ideas. I'll keep quiet, but I want those afternoons with Federico to go on for a long time. Of course, digging in the Cut is not great for Federico, so my idea of prolonging the whole thing serves only me.

"Nature will have to give in to us," Father says, and I come out of my reverie.

"I guess it will."

He gives me the atta-girl wink.

Sixty-five

BUT NATURE DOES NOT GIVE IN.

A week later there are Commission men examining the deep cracks in the ground along the rim of the Cut near the houses, some cracks a few feet from the edge, others as much as a hundred yards back. Our house seems fairly stable, but a crack runs beside a neighbor's house and they're told to leave.

"Not gonna do it." This is the man of the family speaking, a thick, tough crane man. "No crack gonna scare me off my property." "His" property belongs to the Commission, but the defiance is entirely his own. He won't leave.

Father knows geology and engineering and takes the warning seriously. Lives are threatened here, so he tries to explain using logic based on solid geology, thinking a sturdy fellow won't deny sturdy thinking.

"You've got sedimentary and igneous intrusions there," he says to him as a friend and good neighbor. "And it's mixed with the lava flows, and once you disturb that, adhesion's lost." He points at what he's talking about as they stand on our back porch after work.

"See that blue-green volcanic sediment?" The crane man nods. "That'll slip on those red and black clays, lateral support'll be gone, and the slide will start. No stopping it. The house and everybody in it will go down."

The crane man gives Father a blank look and shakes his head. "I'm not leaving."

I see Father's wheels turning. He understands this brute of a fellow and he respects him, but the fellow is allowing his family to be in danger and that's hard for Father to take. He tries again—something simpler, more graphic.

"See the big block of earth where your house is—see how it's splitting away?" A nod. "It'll go any day now, the house with it."

A thoughtful hesitation from the crane man. Then a shake of the head. It's a matter of stern manly stuff now. He won't leave.

Father respectfully goes quiet. The two of them stand staring at the house perched at a tilt. Silent observation—very Midwestern.

A week later, early morning, before it's light, there's commotion outside my window. I get up, look out.

Father's down there, about to leave for work, talking to the crane man, whose back steps have separated from the house and are now well on their way to the bottom of the Cut. As they speak, a rocking chair on his porch tips and tumbles, the earth giving way a bit more.

"Your family's in danger," Father calls to him across our properties in a firm voice of warning.

"You have to leave," Mother says. She sounds scared for them. "Come here—we have room."

Sixty-six

A MEMORABLE TIME, THAT HOUR. We all sit around the kitchen table with coffee and hot biscuits, talking about the situation, slathering on butter and raspberry preserves. I love it. New voices and laughter in our house at such an early hour, a whiff of danger hovering over the warm smell of coffee, the earth moving outside the door.

"The Commission will take care of everything," Father says. The crane man knows this but he still doesn't like it. Father reassures him: "New house, better than that one. They'll move you and you won't miss a day's work."

Father passes him the basket of warm biscuits, making this comfortable for him—he'd be doing the right thing to move, not the cowardly thing. The crane man eats, deep in slow consideration. His timid wife and their little girl no more than ten with long, dark pigtails sit beside his massive frame and wait for a decision. The crane man's hand is so beefy, it's difficult for him to hold the dainty handle of Mother's china cup. The sound of splitting wood halts our talk and we peer out. One of the braces under their porch has started to go, the dirt crumbling under it and moving in narrow flows down the slope. Watching this, the crane man relents.

"Well . . . I s'pose . . ."

"Good," says Father and gets on the phone.

He's relieved. This was a tragedy waiting to happen and it's been averted. Father wants nothing like this on his watch, not when there's safety monitoring by the Commission and preventative measures. It's not necessary. I realize how well taken care of Mother and I are. We're safe, thanks to Father's care. He's good at it. *Don't let me ever shame or disappoint him.*

In a few hours West Indians swarm in, packing, lifting, carrying. By noon furniture is removed, plants taken out, a bicycle and two pet cats placed on a wagon. In less than twenty-four hours the crane man and his family are our neighbors no more—they're in a new house farther back from the edge of the Cut. Their old house moves down the hill in stately disobedience the following night.

As we discuss the matter at supper the next evening, two engineers come to the door.

"Would you step outside," one says to Father.

They've taken core samples, done testing. "You'll need to move right away."

It shouldn't be a shock—we're on the same unstable ground as the neighbor—but Mother stiffens and goes speechless for a moment, looking as though the earth has already dropped out from under her. Father is pragmatic, of course. It's our turn and he says the same things to her that he said to the crane man: "They'll take care of everything. We'll get a better house . . ."

"Yes, I know," she says, but she's angry.

She finishes her meal frowning. They'll enter her home, her private world, and touch her things, handle her possessions—a personal offense to Mother. For her the move will be a challenge.

Two days later we're in another almost identical two-story home—standard Commission architecture, upper and lower screened porches with rockers, a larger living room, a better kitchen, and located farther back from the Cut. It's an airier, more pleasant home, and Mother is relieved. She's happy. She sets to work arranging it exactly to her liking, and I know she'll spend weeks, months at it, organizing each corner, each shelf, the placement of each plant exactly as she thinks best.

None of it matters to me. The move was a pleasant distraction is all. And my new room is bare like the old one, not a trace of childhood. Good.

Federico is still tattooed inside my brain.

Sixty-seven

HE'S NEVER LEFT.

Our first evening in the new house is two weeks after last seeing Federico. He works until four and I'm either at school or home. Art class is over. He's not avoiding me—it's that we've made no new meeting arrangements and I'm not at all sure how things will go.

At the new house on that first evening Mother unwraps cups and saucers in her larger kitchen. Harry, Father, and I sit in rockers on the porch looking out over the Cut. It's farther away now, at a safe distance but still in plain sight.

Harry is still a regular visitor. Father likes his Midwestern ways, and Mother appreciates that he's polite without fail and never uses harsh language or raises his voice. And he's sharp; she has great respect for his intelligence.

I love being around him, but in my mind he's pretty much eclipsed by Federico and everything that's gone on between us. I still manage to do good schoolwork, but more than ever Federico is in my head. I see our bodies together, hear the jungle sounds, replay our urgency and release to the scholarly backdrop of recitations on the Holy Roman Empire or the first winter in

Jamestown—Captain Smith, his mates, their problems. It's all made more vivid by the grip of Federico on my thoughts. I'm not slowed. I make no effort to get him out of my head.

"The Commission took care of everything, didn't it?" Harry says that first evening in the new house. He's propped his feet on our new porch railing.

"We hardly lifted a finger," says Father and looks across the canal, pleased.

I tip back my rocker a little, one leg on the railing. Of course I'm thinking of Federico—the constant visual replay.

"Perfect Socialist model," says Harry. "Largest enterprise going on in the world—taking care of everybody, and not one man at any level working for profit. That's socialism."

I rock and consider his idea. I see it through Federico's eyes; he's already on fire with that idea or something like it for Spain. Interesting.

"Take the Panama Railroad—government run, efficient, never late, always in perfect repair . . . No U.S. railroad's that good or equipped with better safety devices. And the workers, the ones in the Cut—no private contractor in the world is feeding workers any better."

Father interrupts him. "Well now, wait. That's not true. They gave those Spanish fellas bad meat. They had to come to me for help."

"But it was corrected, wasn't it? It hasn't happened again." Father nods. "No problem admitting mistakes and making corrections."

"May be," says Father, and rocks.

"Government runs the Tivoli, the ships between New York and Colon, the commissaries, health care, transportation—everything government run and efficient."

He's right, of course, but I'm watching the magenta sky turn purple, then deep blue, heading toward soft black, Federico hovering in those hues.

"Know what will happen when the canal's built and you go back?" he says.

"What's that?"

"The Socialist party is going to pursue you."

That makes Father chuckle. "What do they want with me?"

"They want you to join up." Father laughs again but Harry is serious. "They think they can get you to vote for the government to take over and run things the way they've run them here. It's true."

"Well, they won't get my vote," Father says. "Things are fine the way they are."

Now Harry laughs. "I thought so. You're from Missouri, right?"

"Saint Joe."

"I told them—I told them about you. You're well read, you know what's going on, you're an informed voter, but you're not from the old country, so you don't have nightmares of wars and marauders . . . They'll never get you or anybody like you on board. You're American, happy enough the way you are."

Harry has a big smile and Father is nodding, and I can just see Federico in this conversation—the energy, the enthusiasm, the contained rage about injustice, leaning against the porch railing, bent toward Father to make a point.

Harry says, "You know who the Socialists found on the payroll last week?"

"Who?"

"A mechanic. Been on the dig from the start, member of the Socialist party. He straightened them around, all right. He told them government ownership doesn't mean a damn thing unless the workers run the government, and in the Zone they sure don't. He ruined their whole theory. Just blew it away!"

Harry chuckles—he loves all this—and rocks. If only Federico were here, he'd get a new idea about Americans. He'd like Harry, already does. And Father—everybody likes Father.

I have to wonder if Ruby McManus is in Harry's mind the way Federico is in mine—her physical presence, skin and soft hair and desire crowding out everything else. I don't think so.

Harry is consumed with socialism and he's making his point, while across from us I see Federico in the last fading streaks of light. Stars are coming out over the hills.

Sixty-eight

HARRY IS ON A ROLL. He doesn't stop.

". . . the Zone's the furthest thing from socialism," he says. "We're divided into castes, very Hindu. Every workman's on a different salary. We're housed and furnished and treated right down to the last item according to our caste . . ." A nod toward Mother's chinking sounds inside. "Size of kitchen, number of electric lights, candlepower, style of bed, size of bookcase . . . you know how it works." A nod from Father. Harry isn't seeing Ruby in his mind; he's absorbed in what he's saying.

My foot drops off the railing. I prop it up again.

". . . Goethals, he's in a palace compared to this. That's not pure socialism. Heads of departments have palatial homes, bosses like you live in furnished homes like this one, and on down . . ."

I make no further effort to clear away the images of Federico and me together on the cot, in the dribbling shower, across his table, against the wall and the hammock, in the afternoon heat for two weeks, and I hear Harry's voice faintly in the background talking to Father. The silhouette of the jungle across the canal is the muscular shape of Federico's shoulders over me and I can't take my eyes away; cries of monkeys and parrots stab the dark.

". . . your quartermaster at two hundred twenty-five dollars is friendly with a station agent making one seventy-five, but their wives would never think of calling on each other socially—that's caste. Engineers and crane men earn different salaries and they don't mix. And the wife of a foreman making one sixty-five has a dining table that's six inches longer than the others and her ice-box holds one more cold storage chicken, so she wouldn't think of sitting down to bridge with a woman whose husband makes one fifty." Harry's really enjoying this. "And I'll tell you something else: none of these women giving their five o'clock teas with two servants is going to like going back to the States and doing her own laundry again with no one to help."

My head tilts back against the rocker. The dark male shoulders of the jungle fade for a moment. Could Harry be right? Mother doesn't indulge in these petty social competitions—they're beneath her. I realize I'm thinking more freely, more openly. It's Federico's embrace that's done it to me, his sexual fit in my body and the heat of him. Opened me right up. I'll never be the same. Thank goodness. I'm more tolerant and forgiving and less critical—I can feel it in these few minutes. I want to defend Mother against what Harry says, stand up for her—this is totally new. How small her annoying peculiarities and how admirable her larger moral code seem to me suddenly. Mother's fine, perfectly all right the way she is.

"I don't think Mother will mind," I say to Harry.

"Maybe," he says.

I know I can't tell Mother about Federico and me, ever, but I have a new respect for her integrity and the rules she holds herself to as firmly as she does me and Father. I like them. She tolerates no petty social competition, no lying that she knows of, no sloth, no silliness, and certainly nothing to indicate a lack of character, and all those are reasonable rules of conduct—they're wonderful ones. All right, they lack the warmth that a love of life could give them, but that's beyond her and no business of mine. They're the family code and a good one, and sitting there on the porch with Father and Harry, I like our code very much. I like us. What's drained out of me is the tormented, twisting, angry, frustrated, unknowing need to escape, and it's left me with plenty of open space to become . . . something else.

I have to take a breath, look around.

I lean forward in my rocker and my new tolerant self asks Father: "Is that true, all that competition among the women?"

"I don't know," he says. "But the canal's getting built."

"No doubt about it," says Harry.

We go quiet again and rock.

This feels so good—no anger or bitterness about Mother, and Federico's face floating in my head. He's making me a better person. I never knew such a thing was possible.

We look out over the darkness, torches lit here and there.

Father clears his throat and stretches his legs.

"Well, it'll be the greatest accomplishment by man on earth," he says.

I wait for Harry to mention the pyramids but he doesn't.

We rock without talking anymore, my mind drifting through shameless images of Federico and me, and I make no effort to stop them.

From inside, the small chinking sounds continue as Mother arranges her kitchen.

Sixty-nine

THIS IS SERIOUS. I have to get in contact with Federico again. We're lovers. It shouldn't be difficult.

I'm lightning fast at schoolwork—assignments done early, always high marks, reading and homework completed on my daily train trips with papers and notebooks scattered on the seat beside me. Outside, Mount Hope, Tiger Hill, Barbacoas, Emperador glide by, but I rarely glance up. Don't notice the deepening Cut or the continuing slides. Dredging is now a regular part of the dig. I don't give much thought to the mounting number of dead and injured—we're told it's at a rate fully commensurate with the immensity and progress of the project. Good. Great. But all that is separate from my secret personal life.

One of my geography reports is called "The Pacific Sunrise Seen in Panama." It's the only country in the Americas where the Pacific coastline hooks around and for a short distance faces east.

Mrs. Ewing thinks it's wonderful, original, and well written. Should I tell her why? That I'm inspired by afternoons with Federico, lying on his cot, lazy, mind numbed? The "warmth" she reads in my essay is carnal.

"You have such passion in your writing, dear," she says.

No kidding.

Federico comes by the hotel on a Sunday and finds me. We're back on track. We begin meeting again at odd times, with new excuses for Mother. We're still a couple.

Harry has finished his enumerating and is now a Zone policeman carrying a Colt .45, keeping order. He can no longer be a cover. My subterfuge is more elaborate and, comfortable with my new lies, I feel no guilt. I'm not hurting anybody, and because I make sure I'm not caught, Mother won't be embarrassed. I'm constantly on guard and make no slips. My life is my own. Eighteen, in my last year of high school, and I feel adult, separate from my parents. I have filled my diary with pages of detailed descriptions of sex with Federico. Those pages are written by an adult. I am on my own, though my parents don't know it.

The subject of Taboga comes up at dinner one night.

Seventy

"WE REALLY SHOULD GO AGAIN," Mother says. Father spears a bite of chicken croquette.

I hardly register this conversation. I've been to Taboga—it's nice but I have no further interest. Federico is not there.

It's a little Pacific island purchased by the U.S. government from the French, cleaned up, repaired, and painted for Americans who are recuperating from illness or just need rest from canal work, a holiday. They've improved the boat landing, removed a slaughterhouse from the beach, and built a lodge. It's been made into a playground for Zoners—we've been there twice. I listen absently as Mother says we need to get away again. I certainly don't.

"It's been almost a year without a break," she says to Father, "and you're looking haggard."

It's true. I've noticed. He's tired and strained from the escalating problems with slides, the top of the canal a good quarter of a mile wider after the recent ones. The movement of tracks and reorganization of trains is increasingly difficult and under more trying conditions. He could use the rest.

But Father balks. He loves what he's doing. He looks forward to each day, takes pride in his work, his accomplishments visible every evening, measurable as workers go to the roundhouse for the next day's assignment. The tracks move farther, deeper, closer to the Pacific, a scalable advance, and it's rewarding. Father is a part of this and he hasn't forgotten the years it took to get there—the relentless but tactful pleading. He doesn't want to miss a minute. Is she crazy? He doesn't say that, of course, but I'm sure he's thinking it.

"You need a rest." Mother is pressing him in her I'm-going-to-prevail tone of voice.

Father knows the tone but doesn't give in. This kind of thing between them is entertaining. I haven't seen it in a long time and never with my new tolerance. Father uses his knife to plaster a small amount of rice on his fork, banking it against the croquette.

Mother continues. "Do you remember the wonderful lush growth and the crescent bathing beach? And Hotel Aspinwall— those beautiful high-ceilinged rooms and wide-open windows so cool and clean and quiet, with no responsibility . . . You need that."

He listens, says nothing, eats.

"And the pineapple and crusty bread and Coca-Cola we bought in the pink bakery. Remember that blue filigreed balcony? Just the strangest thing but so pretty . . ."

What's she doing? Seducing him? This is new. I perk up and listen. What could have happened on that balcony after the Coke and crusty bread? Father concentrates on his food.

"All those wonderful wide corridors and verandas where we can lounge and watch the boats for hours, the big ships leaving Balboa, the oil tankers, passenger steamers, the beautiful yachts . . ." Mother's pitching this trip to him but Father's hardly looking at her. I've never seen them do this. I eat, barely glance at them, act as though I don't hear or care about it.

". . . the spires of Panama City off in the distance. Surely you'd enjoy that again. The pearl shells on the cathedral tower . . ."

"I remember," he says. He wants her to stop.

But she goes on and mentions in passing the new president, Porras. Father looks up quickly and swallows.

"Porras?"

"Yes. He's there. Resting before he's sworn in, I guess." She's stumbled onto something.

"Porras there?"

Belisario Porras, Panama's president-elect, interests Father. He followed the campaign closely. Corruption was accused on both sides, but generally Father favored Porras. He read quotes to us from his speeches in the *Canal Record* and talked to the other bosses about him. Father's face is now alert and bright.

"Well, if he's there . . ."

"Oh, he is, yes," says Mother, and that's it, no further discussion necessary. I think Father imagines he might meet and talk to Porras, but whatever he's thinking, the Taboga trip is on. They'll be leaving for a week.

I lose interest in Mother's seductive ways because this, I recognize in a split second, is a brilliant opportunity.

"Could I stay with Janet or Marion?"

Seventy-one

ARRANGEMENTS ARE MADE. I'll be at school most of the day and with Janet's family at night, only coming to the house each afternoon to check on things, mail, et cetera. Perfect. The late afternoon is all I need. They'll leave in a week and once again my after-school time will be for Federico. It's too good to be true.

I meet Federico at the Tivoli, bursting with my plan. I can't wait to tell him—the house to ourselves every afternoon for a week, like our time in his cabin, only better. We'll have an icebox and a kitchen and a soft bed—a large one if we dare use Mother and Father's room—a whole house to ourselves. But he's solemn and remote and hardly looks at me as I talk. He seems disinterested.

I'm baffled. We're on the best possible terms. I don't understand. "Just an idea . . ." I say.

"It's a wonderful idea, really . . ." But he's distant and I can't figure it out. He takes my hand and says, "Come on."

We walk along the tracks in the dark of evening and he asks me more about the plan, straining to be civil, trying to be normal. When we come to the Tivoli gazebo so hidden and overgrown after the heavy rains, we have to search for it. We are surely the only ones who ever come here. He leads me inside. We sit on a small bench that tilts slightly toward one end. He puts an arm around me and holds me in a friendly way, not at all sexual. He's frowning and several times I think he'll start talking. Maybe I'll hear about his life, what really brings him to this hellish dig, something personal, which, for all our intimacy and his stories of Spanish politics, is still missing. But he doesn't manage to talk—only makes the effort several times, then hugs me close instead and looks out across the canal. Finally he smiles and comes out of whatever is bothering him.

"When do they leave?"

"In four days—this weekend."

"You're counting the days?"

"Of course."

He looks at me as though he hasn't seen me all evening. He unbuttons my blouse and peels it away, rolls the camisole straps off my shoulders. He takes away the layers of my clothing, damp with perspiration and warm. Music from the hotel and occasional laughter filter into our secret place. He keeps his eyes on me, on my arms and breasts, then on my waist and belly when I'm naked in the shadows. He looks at me still smiling.

"What a perfect girl you are, do you know that?"

"I'm eighteen . . ." And as the full-grown woman I feel myself to be, I untie his loose cotton trousers, push them down, and pull him against me.

He catches his breath and we lie down, serious now. This is not playful erotic love, not like at his cabin. There's something desperate in our connection, like the first time we made love in that hidden place, and it overwhelms me. Again. I love his lean body and the care he takes in his sex with me, no matter how desperate its source, and we load that place with our lust, oblivious of heat and rough ground and voices above us—the sexual freight is so great, I know I'll never be able to pass there again without a shudder.

But it's no place to lie together and talk afterward. We could be found, and there are bugs and stiff dead grass. We dress and he helps me reassemble myself, and then he walks me to my house and watches as I climb the steps.

The plan is made. The following Friday after work, he'll come directly to our house, knock on the door, and I'll answer.

Alone.

A Spanish Tale

Seventy-two

I'M WAITING. I hear him coming up the steps and give the house a last quick check: clean, everything in place, cold chicken in the icebox with our other favorite foods; a cool, clean bed upstairs ready for another honeymoon; bigger, better, more commodious this time with every amenity. I smile as he comes through the door. This is going to be great.

"We have to talk," he says. He walks past me, straight into the living room. I follow. "Sit down." He sounds like a professor and I feel like a student called to the principal's office.

"Would you like lemonade or something . . .?"

"No, no. Just sit, please."

I'm perplexed.

His eyes dart around the room as he paces. I ease down onto the edge of the sofa, never take my eyes off him.

"I have to . . . tell you some things." I've never seen him like this. He's usually so assured. He's nervous and wrings his hands. "You don't really know me and that's not right . . . I'm sorry I've let this go so long."

What does he mean? "No reason to be sorry . . ." I say.

"Yes, there is." He's firm, almost irritated.

He keeps pacing and looks around, uncomfortable. Is he a criminal? Why aren't we going upstairs to the bedroom with real bookshelves, a real bed, clean sheets, and a cool breeze? No need to worry about Augusto coming back, no constraints on me, lots of food, a gramophone, a week of self-indulgence, and he's making a tortured effort to speak.

"Let me tell you . . ." He pauses, then plunges in, and it sounds rehearsed. "Alfonso XIII is the king of Spain . . ." I nod, not sure I actually knew that. "He and I were born on the same day, the same year. We didn't know each other; we were just the same age." More pacing. "When he was four, seven other boys and I were chosen to be playmates for him, for his military drills and exercises so he could have a more normal boy's life."

I say that I see but he doesn't hear. "He called us his troop, and I was the one he liked best so we became like brothers. He had two older sisters but he wasn't close to them. Two aunts lived with him; his mother was regent . . ." I look at him, blank. "Alfonso's father died before he was born . . ." Still pacing. "We boys were aristocrats, of course, not *pico y pala* boys. I'm one of the aristocracy—all of us were."

I'm not surprised.

He stands still to see how I'm taking this. I listen. He relaxes a little, then paces again.

"We were pranksters, really unmanageable. Sometimes we'd bungle the military drills on purpose just to humiliate the *teniente* giving orders. That was cruel. We actually apologized to the *teniente* when we were older. I guess we were just being boys, I don't know. We were eight or nine. It's hard to tell when you're so young and isolated from everybody else . . ." I nod, try not to look mystified. "Anyway, the aunties didn't punish us. We were allowed to do anything we wanted, but the troop still had to use the third person with Alfonso. You know, 'Does the king want to play board games or does he prefer a footrace?' As if that's normal. But behind the aunties' backs Alfonso and I were different. We didn't buy into the stupid royal façade. We told obscene jokes, called each other names, broke every rule of decorum we could. It just seemed so absurd. It still does. We hated the stuffy rules and all the phony royal snobbery . . ." Federico sits in Father's Morris chair and that relaxes me a little, but not him. He sits straight as he talks.

"We were going to change the world—that was the plan and it wasn't a childish idea. It was real. He was going to be king. He could do it." He thinks hard, then says, "I don't think anyone ever wanted to change his country as much as Alfonso did when he was young." He looks directly at me for the first time. "Even now I believe that."

"What happened?"

"He just . . . didn't do it."

Seventy-three

"I DON'T KNOW WHY HE DIDN'T. Maybe nobody does. Anyway, when he was sixteen, he was sworn in as king, and I was in the audience of the Cortes, the court, watching the ceremony, and

I remember thinking, 'This is it, the new era—we're going to change everything.' I felt like a giant knowing that. We'd build schools and make the peasants into a strong middle class, make Spain a major European power—everything would change. It was the beginning of a new life . . . or so I thought." He shakes his head, baffled, trying to work it out as he talks. "But it wasn't. Nothing changed except Alfonso and I don't know why."

Federico grinds on this as he talks about it. It still eats at him—I can see it.

"Maybe it happened to him later, after the installation. It could have happened then, in the Church or during the cortege. All that boring pomp—the Te Deum and prayers and hymns and men in robes praying for him and then the scepter . . . But he'd seen that all his life—he wasn't impressed by that. I just . . . I still don't understand it."

He looks at me, at the floor, out across the porch, then back at me again.

It sounds like a fairy tale but I know it isn't. This is his life and it's serious.

"I've been trying to figure it out for ten years," he says and squeezes his temples. He looks at me hard. "You do know this king business is a human invention, don't you? No matter what they tell you about God and anointing, royalty is a human fabrication, some primitive need for a father figure. That's all it is."

I nod and he goes on about that day, how everybody wanted to go home after the coronation and Alfonso wouldn't release them. This was more bizarre to me than the first part of the story. Instead the new king called the ministers for a council of state, which is never done on coronation day.

"Nobody'd ever heard of such a thing, but he did it and the council met and he demanded to know why the military academies had been closed. Can you imagine? A stupid thing like that? Some relic of our military drills that he liked, I suppose, so he calls a special council for that on coronation day? Anyway, the ministers were hot and tired so they said yes, they'd open the academies again if he wanted, and they were ready to leave and he stopped them. Said they weren't released." Then, shaking his head, "He was really barking mad."

"You don't know why?" I'm completely drawn into this now.

"No. No idea. He just went on talking and droning on about being king—one of the ministers told me all about it; I got all the details—then Alfonso read an article out loud from the constitution that gives him the right to confer honors and civil appointments. Pure egomania is what that was, and the ministers were fed up with this upstart, so king or no king, they reminded him he couldn't do anything without their consent, which is in the constitution, too, and they marched out. Good for them." Federico rubs his eyes and shakes his head. "Fool, absolute fool."

"Wasn't there anything you could do?"

He gives that some thought. "You know . . . no. Nothing. But it still wasn't over, this ego attack of the king's. That night at dinner, he ordered his aunt Eulalia to eat cauliflower, which she detested. A king's order, and his mother sent him to bed without his supper like a child, which he still was. Course, it was all over town the next morning, everybody talking about it, the whole story—the fool boy king throwing his weight around with his auntie. The servants couldn't wait to let that one out."

Federico is now lost in this memory, shaking his head, hardly knowing I'm there, but I venture a few words. "Were you still friends?"

"I was still his playmate, yes, but he never mentioned our plans for change, not a word. Can you imagine that? Growing up talking about changing an entire country, a whole sector of Europe, and in one afternoon it disappears. He never mentioned it again, didn't want to hear about it. He'd call me for some sport, polo or a fast auto ride, or maybe to watch a midnight movie—he was always needing a rest from his 'tiring royal duties,' as he called them—but there was never another word about changing Spain."

Federico stands, looks around. "The Church is richer than ever. The poor are dying and he's watching Western movies imported from America." He takes a deep breath, digs his fists into his pockets, and faces me squarely.

"Now, listen to me," he says. "There have been three attempts on Alfonso's life. I organized one."

Seventy-four

SO THIS IS IT, THE BIG REVELATION.

"It failed—he's still healthy." I can't tell if he's ashamed of the attempt or the failure. "It was justified, I promise you."

I nod.

"My brother and I saw a priest in a shop having chocolate with a landowner one afternoon, a rotten, fat bastard who abused his laborers and everybody knew it. Underpaid them or didn't pay them at all, beat them, God knows what else. Course, he paid off the parish to overlook the whole thing—that's what's done over there—and Victor and I were seething at this fat, greedy buffoon sitting there with his priest, chuckling and sipping chocolate, the two of them, Church and State in collusion right in front of our eyes. We were ready to kill them. But we didn't. We wouldn't have. We weren't assassins . . . not yet, anyway." He stops, angry.

"What happened?"

"Officers came. They held me at gunpoint and took Victor away."

"Why not you?"

"Possibly they knew I was part of Alfonso's troop. He may have protected me, given orders not to pick me up, I don't know. Maybe that *teniente* we apologized to when we were boys had something to do with it. I keep trying to figure it out. I'll never know. Anyway, they took Victor to Montjuich and tortured him."

I flinch at that, my first sign of emotion. Federico now keeps his eyes on me, doesn't back off or spare me the details. He wants to see if his little Dayton flower can take a hot wind of Spanish truth and I do take it, looking him straight in the face, no tears, no recoil, unmoving.

"They kept him in the double-zero cells and whipped him, forced him to stay on his feet without sleep for days, and fed him dry bread and salt fish with no water until he vomited blood. But he didn't reveal any names. He didn't give in, and my assassination attempt failed."

He stands still, contains his own emotion.

Slanting rays of setting sun fall across both of us. I don't feel the heat or the breeze from the Cut, only a slight nausea caused by what he's just said and the strain of the situation.

"I came to Panama after that," he says. "My family was afraid I'd be arrested, and Alfonso took all our money and property, everything, calling it a voluntary contribution to the Church. It killed my father, literally. His heart gave out." Tears jump to his eyes. He sucks in his breath.

"And your brother?" I say.

"The torture left him blind and he can't talk. My mother takes care of him. The two of them live in a little room . . . That's all that's left of my father's fortune." A sardonic laugh comes out of him. "The Church took her husband, her son, everything she owned and forced me to leave the country, but my mother still gives pennies to the Virgin when she can and prays. She doesn't grasp it."

He steps onto the porch and looks across the Cut for a moment. "I should have told you this a long time ago."

"You tried, didn't you?"

"Did I?"

"This week in the gazebo?"

"You could tell?"

"We made love instead."

"Right."

The sky is changing from violet to deep blue-black, another spectacular end of a day. "Do you know what the peasants earn?" he says to me, still looking away. "Three shillings six a week. That's what in dollars?" He looks back but he doesn't really want an answer. He just takes another deep breath.

He's shaken and so am I.

"Wouldn't you like something to drink?" I'm amazed at my poise—I guess that's what it is.

"Thank you, no. Really, I'm all right."

We're now officially a universe apart.

In my mind I see our Methodist church on the corner of Twelfth Street—Wednesday prayer meetings, Thursday carry-in supper, no ornaments, a picture of a Nordic-looking Jesus with wavy brown hair, no rituals, hymns, prayers, and a sermon about right living and staying clean of soul. The collection plate is passed—give if you can . . .

"I can't imagine it," I say.

"That's good." He smiles, his head tipped a little to the side. He likes that about me. Reading *El Unico* is as close as I'll come to his deranged world. Our house is as close as he'll come to my benign one. He stands there, pensive, looking at me, then says, "I can't stay, I'm sorry . . ."

He glances around the room and understands that he's destroyed my plans. "I'm sorry, really."

"I understand."

He looks at me in that curious way again, trying to figure me out, as though he doesn't know me or my kind and wants to but not right now, no time for that now.

He nods—no courtly bow—we're way past that.

He goes toward the kitchen and I follow. Out on the porch he pushes the screen door open, smiles at me weakly, and goes down the steps. He doesn't look back again and his figure disappears behind the brush along the track.

Seventy-five

WHEN HE'S OUT OF SIGHT I GO BACK IN and sit on the sofa, looking out at the darkness that's descended in only minutes.

My eyes finally rest on the table beside Father's chair, where there are clippings from Katharine's latest letter about Orville's recent European trip and with it newspaper photos of the flying machine tipped at a slight angle in the sky. I stare at it from across the room. There's an index card lying with the letter. Katharine's sent the recipe for Orville's turkey stuffing so we won't have to go another Christmas without it. She knows how much we all love it, and Mother, who rarely asks anyone for anything, has requested that recipe, and there it sits while they're in Taboga.

I take the card into the kitchen and put it with Mother's other recipes in alphabetical order in a small blue box with a faded floral design on the hinged top. I push the recipe box back into its place and stand there trying to take in what has just happened, but I can't. It doesn't seem real. It's a story from another world that I'm not likely to ever see.

What is real and clear to me is that Federico and I are now further apart.

I cannot write a single word about this in my diary that night, and I don't see or hear from him again for weeks.

Seventy-six

It's Saturday evening and on the track below us a group of Spaniards appears, carrying two large flags and singing "Garibaldi." Father is the first to hear them. He goes out on the porch to watch.

"Spaniards," he says when I join him. "They have troubles back home, you know."

"Mmm."

Mother comes out with us.

They're almost straight below our house, all of them dressed in colorful clothes, sashes and berets, with flags and banners and a leader—Federico.

I stop breathing. My eyes go wide.

The group stops walking. Federico steps forward, looks up at us, and speaks. I really can't breathe.

"We have come to thank you, *Jefe*. You have been a great help to us in the past and you are our loyal friend . . ." And he goes on—more good things about Father and that they've come to honor him. Mother remarks to me quietly about the quality of Federico's elegant speech.

"Oh, yes," I say and have to clear my throat.

Federico's voice carries well; we hear every word praising Father. There are cheers and shouts of *"Viva!"* Mother and Father watch, completely entertained and I begin to relax a little.

"Good men," Father says. "Good men."

The group suddenly begins climbing our hill. My stomach

screws tight as Federico leads them boldly, not showing the slightest fear.

Father smiles and gives them a little salute in greeting. Federico doesn't avoid looking at me but doesn't give any indication he's ever seen me before, either. He looks very correctly at all three of us, the *jefe*'s family, and focuses on Father, the center of the occasion.

They're halfway up the steps and Federico shouts out political slogans, *viva* this or *a bajo* that, about honor and justice, and the group responds with "*Viva*" to each one. Then the flag bearers come up the steps to cross the flags in front of us, and the group sings a melody about Spain and its natural bounty. I'm terrified and excited and want it to end, but the song goes on and on.

Mother, who usually dislikes demonstrations, loves this, the singing and Federico's handsome face looking up at us.

"He's very good looking," she murmurs to me.

"Mmm."

They finish and there's another shouted *viva* for Father. He gives them his friendly salute again and they retreat down the hill. Federico shoots me a quick glance and I half smile. I'm shaking.

"Beautiful," I say to Mother, trying to be normal.

"I don't ever want to forget that," Mother says. "Oh, the Kodak, for heaven's sakes!" Too late. No snapshots.

We're going back into the house, blood finally pumping through me again, when we hear someone behind us—Augusto.

"Please come with us, *Jefe*," he says. "*A bajo* in the cantina . . . a banquet."

Augusto is not as smooth as Federico. He keeps glancing at me, which Mother notices. She nudges me.

"He sees how pretty you are," she whispers.

Heart pounding, stomach churning. "I'm flattered," I say. This is too much.

Seventy-seven

FATHER GOES WITH THEM TO THE BOTTOM OF THE HILL into the Brown Spider Cantina, a grim establishment nicely decked out for the festivities.

Mother and I sit on the porch and listen to the celebration. The whole thing unnerves me. We bring out plates of supper and eat with the singing and shouts of *"Viva"* and revolutionary speeches drifting up the hill.

There are occasional clear phrases about saving *España*, which I loosely translate for Mother. Spanish is still difficult for her and the voice we hear most is Federico's. For me it's unsettling.

"He speaks so beautifully," says Mother.

Of course he does.

Hours later, long after dark, Father comes back and describes the evening: lots of wine and food he's never seen before.

"Spicy," he says, "and some of it hard to eat. They passed around those leather pouches—the wine streams into your mouth. All kinds of toasts . . . to me . . . to Spain . . . other things. You know, most of them said they'd worked at my site one time or another, but I couldn't remember all their faces. That leader, though, I remember him—fellow named Federico. Nothing like the others." He sinks into a chair, full of food and wine, and says he's dizzy.

This shakes me, hearing Father say Federico's name.

"Their Spanish is too fast for me, but I got the gist of it. Spain must be a mess—starving population, bad king, corruption . . ." He shakes his head. "A shame . . . All of them are good boys, bright. Any one of them could learn to do my job in no time . . . and here they are . . ."

He waves his hand toward the Brown Spider and shakes his head again. He understates his own expertise to show his admiration for the hard-working Spaniards, typical of my modest father. Mother agrees with him and I stay silent, and in a little while the two of them go upstairs to bed.

The noise from the banquet continues, and I can see the edge of the cantina from my room overlooking the foliage and growth down the hill and across the tracks. Among the voices is Federico's, stronger and firmer than the others.

I try to figure out the whole thing. I don't doubt he's planned this ceremony to honor Father, the good-natured American they all work with from time to time who wishes them well, supports them, thinks of them as something more than faceless labor. He's a man to be respected. But in my fevered mind I believe Federico organized the whole elaborate scheme to make his presence known to me again, to make things right, and that's the thought I hold on to because it's what I want to believe: it was all for me.

Different versions of the scenario drift in my head for hours, but one thing sticks: Federico, the leader, the organizer, forced to flee king and country, has boldly stood on our steps leading cheers for Father and facing me with my parents. This is a new version of him that I never expected. It's exciting.

And it creates a new version of me: less secretive, more self-assured, less jumpy.

The next morning I feel stronger and ready for the day, and once again I feel there's nothing I can't do, nothing I can't overcome.

Entry in my diary: *We're a couple again.* That's all.

DETOUR

Seventy-eight

Mr. Herman from the school office comes in with a note for Mrs. Ewing, glances at me, and goes out.

Mrs. Ewing calls me to her desk.

"You have to go home immediately."

"Father's hurt?"

"Heavens no. Something that important, they'd come for you. It must be something else. Don't worry. Go on home."

But Mother's never called me home "immediately" for any reason and I know only something extreme would make her do it. I do worry.

The train ride to Culebra seems endless and so does the walk to our house in air heated to bursting, about to break in a downpour. I imagine awful things—Father hurt, Orville killed, Mother herself sick or injured somehow . . . Up our hill two steps at a time, in the back door.

Mother calls down from upstairs.

"There's a terrible flood."

I bound upstairs and she's hurrying around the bedroom, talking and packing.

"We'll take the twelve-forty to Colon, board the *Advance* tonight. Start packing."

What? *WHAT?*

"Every house on Hawthorne Street's flooded; every structure in Dayton is in deep water. Katharine called and said some of the single-story houses are covered to the roof—it must be terrible . . ."

It *is* terrible. Horrible. Leaving Federico just when things are bound to heat up again. (Not a single thought for my Dayton neighbors.) "This is awful," I say.

"Pack some clothes, something sturdy—there's mud everywhere. The water's deeper downtown than at our house. All the stores on Main are under water and mud on everything. Bring your high-top shoes and jodhpurs. Can you imagine it? Business files floating down Main Street? And chairs and tables. There's furniture floating all over—she said it looks like toys in a bathtub . . ."

All right. Stay calm. Think this through. How will I get word to Federico? I'm about to disappear and he'll have no idea what's happened.

I know the visit honoring Father signified we'll get together soon, but if I'm gone and not at any of our regular meeting places, he won't know what to think. He'll probably think Mother and Father have found out and I'm punished somehow for life. But how do I let him know what's really going on?

". . . it started Sunday. Katharine said you could hardly hear the closing hymn, it poured so hard, but this time of year, you know, there's always rain and some flooding . . . Bring all your underwear—we won't be able to wash easily."

"Why?"

"Everything's under water . . ." She stops and looks at me, frowning. It's pretty obvious I'm rattled but not for the same reason she is.

"Right, right," I say. I duck my head and get busy.

Seventy-nine

It's a disaster of major proportions. It's not one of our standard Ohio Valley spring floods. There are injuries, deaths, and terrible damage. Mother says waters from the Miami and two other rivers rampaged toward Dayton and a dam collapsed, so it was a wild torrent by the time it reached the city. The levee on Stratford Avenue overflowed, flood breaks on East Second and Fifth streets gave way, and the city was inundated. This is biblical.

Mother's agitation doesn't keep her from moving fast, neatly folding her garments and placing them into cases while she advises me what to bring and relays Katharine's news.

". . . she says she and Orville overslept on Tuesday and rushed out to appointments in another part of town, and the flooding happened so fast, they couldn't get back to the house . . ."

I follow her orders, pack what I'll need, but I'm knotted inside and completely stressed.

An hour later we're on the train.

Mother stares out at Zoners as we pass but I don't think she sees them. She's silent, deep in worry. The flood is grinding in her like Federico is in me.

Suddenly she says, "Milton and Mrs. Wagner were rescued by a man in a canoe. Imagine that—took them to Mr. Hartzell's house."

"Incredible," I say.

"Our living room and dining room and kitchen are float-ing . . ."

There's a catch in her throat, and that's the last she says about the flood. She can't go on and I'm glad; she's upset.

Nothing in the Dayton house means much to me, but I know it does to her. The furniture and the pictures on the walls and small articles were carefully chosen and placed, and they're Mother's entire life. I have no attachment to any of it, but I can't keep from feeling for her, and just for a second, Federico is out of my mind. I hug her.

I've never done that before, never been the one to give com-fort to her. She's hurting and fearful, no doubt, of what we'll see when we get to our house half submerged in river water and unlivable, only the upstairs high and dry.

Mother wipes her nose, gives me a quick smile of gratitude, and looks out the window.

It feels good to console her but I'm hating this, every minute taking me farther away from Federico.

That evening we sail for New York.

Eighty

ON THE TRAIN FROM NEW YORK TO OHIO I can only agonize over how long we'll have to stay, still no concern or sympathy for my Dayton neighbors. I don't ask Mother; she couldn't possibly know, and considering the suffering and destruction we're going to see, it's all wrong to mention.

I ride along in a daze of Federico scenarios—him searching for me, giving up, sweating in the Cut, wondering why I've dropped out of sight. No longer his good-natured, totally reliable American girl after all? I shudder at the thought. When we pull into Dayton Station, I look out the window and thoughts of Federico vanish.

Nothing Mother said has prepared me for this: Dayton is submerged in yellow ooze. Fences and hedges are torn and twisted in the mud. It looks like the aftermath of a cyclone, a flood in its wake.

We arrive at Hawthorne Street and it reeks. There are heaps of refuse moldering where flower beds used to be. The Wrights' perfect lawn and rock garden are jumbled with debris and unrecognizable objects.

A tricycle has been deposited with mud against the Wrights' wraparound porch, the one the boys built. Their beautiful turned railings are slime caked and smeared. Porch rockers have all but disappeared, pushed against the wall, plastered with sludge. The expert handwork Orville did on the uprights is covered with silt that's dried to a strange ochre gloss. And near the second floor, a dirty yellow line makes a high-water mark as it does on all the houses on the street—on ours, too.

It's a shock to see.

Our house looks much like the Wrights', with nothing done to clear away the litter packed with mud on our porch. Mother stiffens but doesn't say a word.

We go inside, Mother in high boots and heavy clothing, me beside her with Mrs. Wagner, a neighbor, who warns us, "Slowly—you don't know what's under the mud."

It's a damp, trashed cave. Mud is thick on the floor. Walls are streaked with slime, paper peeled and hanging in strips. Several pictures still hang in place but they're slimed and twisted. The furniture rises from the mud in clumps like the steam shovels under the Cucaracha slide.

Mother looks around and with no sentiment or shock says, "Our work is cut out for us."

She sounds like Colonel Goethals—no self-indulged simpering from her. *Let's get to it.*

We start digging.

Eighty-one

THE GRIM JOB GOES ON FOR HOURS. We lift saturated chairs off the sofa, set tables upright, stand the breakfront back up against the wall. We throw out books; their pages are so swollen, they'll never be readable again. We clear through mess after mess, and Mrs. Wagner, who has already done this at her own house, is cheerful and keeps urging us on.

"It will soon be as pretty as ever, you'll see," she says.

Not a chance.

She's the neighbor who gave me bread and jam when I was little and came to visit her. Those words are more bread and jam, meant to keep us happy. But Mother knows they won't fix a thing. No possibility of putting this back together in a few days.

We arrange for workmen to come, and one by one they show up. They dig and clear inside and out. Whole crews of them are moving through the town. Some of them are part of Dayton's civic maintenance, and others are hired groups or day laborers.

"Everybody gets help whether they can pay or not," says the wiry guy lifting a tree limb in our yard.

It's Dayton's version of West Indian workers in the Zone, and like them, these Dayton men work without complaint. They pull, haul, wash down. They restore order. They're cheerful, too, and optimistic. They are my people in a way Federico or the undulating Panamanian women can't be. I begin to feel that strongly as the hours pass. Dayton doesn't seem so provincial, just good folks helping one another. I've been hard on my hometown. Federico seems very far away and our indulgence seems like . . . indulgence.

At some point late in the morning, after hours of work, Mother says, "Better go next door—get their news." I don't need persuading, and as I turn to go she says, "You should plan on going back. I don't want you missing so much school."

"All right."

With those words joy washes over me and overwhelms my thoughts of homey Dayton. Panama is where I'm adult and myself. Dayton reminiscence is nice, but it means nothing now that I'm older.

I stand at the door watching Mother as she goes back to work on a small china tea set, wiping a cup clean and placing it in a cardboard box. That tea set is old-fashioned to me, the sort of thing I'd never have in my own house—useless decoration. But there it is, still in its place on the table in the living room. That little inanimate piece of our life bravely peeping out through the slime—it looks so helpless, I want to cry. I can't wait to get back to Panama.

Eighty-two

I SET OUT FOR THE WRIGHTS', FEELING GOOD. I try to go the usual route across the little hedge separating our backyards, but that won't work. It's heaped with mud and it's impossible to tell what's under there or if I'll hurt myself plunging knee-deep into ooze. I go the front way, where workers have used snow shovels to expose sidewalks and paths.

Orville is in the kitchen.

"Well, well," he says.

He's hardly changed. It's been almost three years since I've seen him. I was fifteen; now I'm eighteen—child to woman.

"Everything seems smaller." I have to laugh.

"You're larger," he says. We sit at the kitchen table. "The Bishop's helping across town."

"Katharine and Carrie?"

"They're at church dispensing food and water."

I look around at the kitchen, cleared and clean and usable, electricity restored, refrigeration, running water—just like the Wrights to be the first on the block back in working order.

"How's your father?" he asks.

"Good. And loving his work."

He asks about Mother and says he'll step over and say hello to her later.

"So little's changed," I say. He nods.

We talk, find some dried apricots, and Orville makes coffee. He isn't wearing his starched collar—he's in a flannel shirt and boots like everyone else.

"We're all in strange getups these days," he says.

"And how about the machines?" Our common interest. "Are they okay?"

"The ones at the factory are fine, but everything here and at the shop is gone. Total loss . . ." He shakes his head mostly in bewilderment. "You never saw anything like it—be glad you were gone. And how do you like it down there?"

"Very much. I didn't at first—you know, nobody interesting. Nobody building flying machines, anyway."

"I don't know why not—they're doing it everywhere else."

"So I hear."

"And using our plans. Course, we're working on the patents. Judge Hazel decided against Curtiss, so he can't continue, but he's filing an appeal."

"Are patents so difficult?"

"They are."

He looks me over and smiles, that wise, quizzical Wright

smile. He sets down his coffee. "You grew up," he says. "You're a grown, calm woman."

I laugh, a little nervous. Something about Federico shows? "Wasn't I calm before?"

"No. You don't remember? Wil always said if we could harness your energy, we'd fly."

"I didn't know that. I thought I was just your mascot."

"You were, a good one. But we don't need a mascot anymore —do you have any lawyering skills?"

I laugh, pop another apricot in my mouth, sip coffee. Orville says, "Got home from Europe last Wednesday thinking my only problems were legal ones, then Sunday the rains started and there were fires from gas escaping all over the city. You could see them from Summit Street. It looked like the bicycle shop and all of Third Street were blazing, but it was the big buildings west of Third, not ours. All our aeronautical papers were saved."

"And the photos?"

"Some of them are gone. Everything downstairs and at the shop is a total loss . . . The data on our work survived, though, and the plate John Daniels exposed just after the machine lifted off the first time"—I nod—". . . only lost a corner of that. The image wasn't damaged."

A famous photo—the flier tilted, lifting off, a few people watching. It's saved and I'm glad. It was the beginning of everything for me that day—my ninth birthday, the letter from Panama, Federico. That day is saved forever in the photo of the first flight.

"How is it, you being president of the Wright Company?" I ask.

A grimace. "It's got to be done." He looks away for a minute.

"I miss him. I keep thinking he'll walk in the door. Do you know I thought of you when he was sick?"

"Why me?"

"They thought it was malaria at first, and you've got it licked down there, don't you?"

"Yes."

"But then Dr. Conklin said he thought it was typhoid fever, which I had before you were born and got through it, and it scared Wil into being more careful of contaminated food and water . . . It's ironic he'd get it and not survive."

"Wish I'd been here."

"It was a service just the way he wanted. Then, when they lowered him into his grave, church bells rang and everything stopped—streetcars, autos, everything. People stopped walking and bowed their heads. After that they came and piled flowers on the porch—the paper said thousands but I didn't keep count. They were bringing flowers day and night. I don't think you would have liked the traffic." A wry smile, then he brightens and says, "One more thing."

Eighty-three

I FOLLOW HIM UPSTAIRS. No water has reached there—everything is exactly the same. In the Bishop's room Orville takes his father's diary from a bedside table, finds a page, and reads:

"Wilbur was forty-five years, one month, and fourteen days old. A short life, full of consequences. An unfailing intellect, imperturbable temper, great self-reliance and modesty. He lived and died seeing the right clearly and pursuing it steadfastly."

He closes the diary and replaces it. "He wouldn't mind you hearing that."

No, he wouldn't.

These are my people. Always.

A wave of something goes through me—sadness, maybe, and a little shame for thinking Dayton less worthy than Panama, or anywhere else, for that matter. Orville is winning me back without knowing it or trying.

We go out to the shed. The 1903 flier is in the corner.

"We had it stowed behind the shop, and so much mud covered the crates it was protected."

"Amazing."

"It's pretty much strips of wood now, but it's the one that flew, so I guess we'll hang on to what's left of it."

"I just stopped wearing the dress Mother made from the wing fabric."

"That right? Mrs. Tate made dresses for her girls, too, I believe. We burned the other gliders, had to make room for the new ones."

He pulls out several glass-plate negatives, holds them up to the light that filters into the shed, some emulsion starting to peel at the corners, and there it is, the crew at the U.S. Lifesaving Service Station at Kill Devil Hill—seven rough-looking men in caps with mustaches and coats, looking with severe manliness toward the camera.

"Is Mr. Daniels there?" I ask.

"That's him." He points him out. "Surfman Daniels." Then

he holds up the plate Daniels made of the first flight, hardly damaged. "The one picture he ever took."

The dark, tilted shape of the two wings lifting off the rails, Wilbur to the side. "Wil told the men to holler and clap and try to cheer me when I started down the rails."

"Did they?"

"I don't know. I just remember lifting off—we had good winds that day . . ." He remembers the winds.

First time—the machine airborne, Wil at awkward midstride. It's my day, too, captured on that murky plate—my birthday, the first mention of Panama.

"Wil looks a little startled, doesn't he?" Orville says, classic Wright humor.

He carefully puts the plate away.

The next day I'm on the train headed back to Federico.

HOME

Eighty-four

MIDAFTERNOON, PANAMA RAIN DRENCHING ME, and I'm anxious.

I climb the steps to the Ancon Police Station hoping to find Harry, but Federico's the only thing on my mind—how to patch things up after my absence.

My head rises into view and so does Harry's—he's sitting in a swivel chair, gazing out over his domain, another officer working at a desk behind him.

"Look at you," he says.

I'm in jodhpurs and high-top shoes still caked with Dayton mud, just off the 12:20 train. I'm out of breath and bursting with eagerness.

"Just got back," I say. I'm panting and plop down in a chair beside him.

"Your father told me you were gone. Flood, right?"

"Yeah, terrible."

"Spring flood?"

"Worse. To the second story of our house. Haven't you been reading about it?"

"Some."

"It's the worst in a hundred years . . ." I'm uneasy and jumpy, wanting to contact Federico, so I start rattling on about cleanup and Orville's pursuit of patents, and it knocks Harry out that I know the Wrights. I describe Mother's pursuit of salvageable items. "She'll be there another two or three weeks . . ."

He pours ice water for us and I press the glass to my neck and face, but it doesn't help much. I'm jittery and hot.

It's hard to focus, so I ask Harry how police work suits him.

"I like it, but I'll tell you something . . ." And I realize I've made a mistake. He's about to go off on one of his long rambles and I don't think I'll be able to stand it, not now, not while I'm fidgeting about Federico.

I tighten, try to calm myself and listen, but I can tell he's going to be thorough. He is:

Number of men in the police force
Police force security measures
How the force is organized
Caste system in the force

My mind is ticking off my own list: ways to reach Federico.

Go to his cabin after the last whistle (but I can't explain that to Father, who'll be expecting me at home).
Go to his cabin after dark (but Father won't let me out alone at night).
Any one of several old ploys (but I can't lie to Father, not like I do to Mother).

Now I really am going crazy. I shift, glance around, tune back in to Harry.

". . . strange case we're on now—interesting, too, but I don't know what to make of it. A murderer's out there and we haven't caught him."

"Really?"

"What a wicked history of violence in this strip of jungle." Oh, God, he's going to start again.

"Worse than anywhere else?" I say. I'm thinking of straight out asking Harry about Federico, say I'm going to do a paper on Spanish workers and have to interview him, which is a good idea, a great one I should have thought of before. Harry knows Federico would be a good subject because he doesn't fit the worker mold. Is there some way I can discreetly bring it up?

Eighty-five

". . . Pizarro and his rousters off to conquer South America from here—rape and pillage, that's what that was."

"Right . . ."

"And Morgan, the old buccaneer, he burned the city to the ground—tide came in and drowned the prisoners. And in those hills over there"—Harry nods across the canal—"did you know men died trying to carry a ship across the Isthmus?" He laughs and I do, too, half-heartedly. (I've got to ask about Federico.) "The old Spanish viceroys cruised right by 'em on palanquins, thought they were fools. Those old boys didn't care—they knew it was a bloody jungle. And what else . . ." I'm not sure how long he'll go on or if I can take it. "Balboa's head was axed off somewhere there—that was after he killed a few thousand himself. You keeping count? He got here stowed away in a cask—bet you didn't know that."

I grin, shift in my chair. I wonder why I haven't thought of "interviewing" Federico before—a great, aboveboard deceit.

". . . even the forty-niners left their bones out there, and they didn't find much in the way of gold. Then the French died wading around with survey kits, thousands of them, and now us. Of course, we're taking death regular as a clock." He turns to me. I open my mouth to speak. "You're going to see it finished, you know," he says.

"Excuse me?"

"In a few months they'll blast the last dam and let the water through, and that first ship'll glide in the rainforest like some amphibious monster. You'll see it."

He doesn't take his eyes off me. It's the same look I got from Orville two weeks earlier—a gaze that comes from nowhere—and in the same breath, as though it's a part of his bloody-Isthmus history, Harry says, "You've grown up."

"People don't grow up overnight." I brush it off, look across the canal, feigning unconcern. There's no way to bring up Federico now—it would sound out of place. "What's the interesting case?"

"Ah, Malero. Do you remember the Spanish fellow with the shelf full of philosophy books?"

Dead air for a second, and then I manage, "Uh-huh."

"We've got him."

"Got him?" Through dry lips.

"For assault. Of course, it's ridiculous."

My voice almost cracks. "He assaulted somebody?"

"Course not, he's not a brawler. He told me he's here to get literary material, but I figured that out from the books on his shelf. You remember the cabin?"

"I think so."

"Says he has no interest in the social life on the canal. He's too busy writing and reading, doesn't drink, doesn't dance, doesn't want to squander time on frivolities—his word, *frivolities*—but he wanted to see one of those wild Saturday night debauches on the edge of the jungle. It's funny when he tells about it—sounds like he's right out of Oxford . . ."

"Really?" I've recovered and switch to my brightly interested voice.

"Better English than us. So he goes to a drunken dance in the Miraflores bush and the usual riot breaks out, and there's a revolver and some shots, and now there's a Peruvian mulatto up in the hospital shot in the mouth, the bullet lodged in his neck. He says Malero did it."

"Couldn't be."

"Course not. Anyway, the morning after this fiasco—I hadn't even heard about it—I strolled in here and there was Malero, quiet as a monk, couldn't shoot a rabbit . . . You remember him?"

"I think I do, yes . . ."

"I had to take him to the hospital to be identified by the Peruvian. He's sitting up there on his cot with his face swollen, can't swallow and has to spit into a cup, can't even talk. And he takes one look at Malero and says he's the one. Actually, he wrote it down because he can't talk. But he wasn't sure—I could tell, he just wants to pin his misery on somebody. Anyway, I kept after him and he finally wrote down he couldn't be certain and that's his final statement."

"What can you do?"

"I have to hold Malero until I can clear him somehow."

I'm together now, cool as anything. "I'll speak to Father."

"About this?"

"He knows him."

"He knows Malero?"

"He knows all the Spanish workers. He knows Malero well." I tell him about the festival honoring Father, the Spanish visits to our house, and that Father's their *jefe*. "He'll gladly vouch for Federico."

Harry jumps up. "Why did you let me rattle on about the jungle?"

"I didn't know you had Malero . . ."

But he's checking his watch. "Let's go," he says, and we bolt out the door.

Halfway down Ancon Hill the sultry heat turns to saturating rain.

Eighty-six

WE TOWEL OURSELVES DRY and Harry chucks wood into our cookstove. I chop vegetables and carve up leftover beef from a generous neighbor. I'll return the favor as soon as I get to the commissary. I make a fine stew and work the flour and butter together for biscuits and toss a salad. I'm good at this. We move fast and chat, though nothing more is said about Federico. I'm excited but calm, too, like the first time I talked to Federico. Strange how that is.

After a while, just as it happens every day with Mother, Father comes up the steps. "I smelled it halfway up—" he says, and then he sees Harry. "Harry! Well, I declare . . . good to see you."

At the table stew and steaming vegetables are passed around. The warm biscuits are tucked in a basket under a napkin, and we help ourselves to chunks of butter and ladle gravy.

Father wants to hear from me about the flood, the condition of our house, how Mother's holding up. Harry doesn't mention Federico; he knows Father should hear about his flooded home first.

"She's fine, working all day," I say. "Sludge and slime are on everything. Downtown water was up to the second stories. Our downstairs is pretty wrecked. She's not discouraged, though— Mrs. Wagner is helping." He's heard most of this already from Mother by phone.

"Is she eating right? You know how she'll forget to eat."

"Katharine's seeing to that, says they have supper together." Father misses her, I can tell. He isn't himself without her.

I can't bear it anymore and I say to Harry, "Tell him about Federico."

"Ah, yes . . ." Fork down, elbows on the table. He leans forward. "I understand you know this fella, Federico Malero."

"Why, sure . . ."

"Well, you won't believe this story . . ." Harry tells him what happened and Father shakes his head in disbelief. "You know looking at him the Spaniard couldn't have done it."

"Course not. He's a first-rate fella."

"Will you vouch for him so I can cut him loose?"

"Why, sure. That's the craziest thing I've ever heard of. That boy has no more business in a jail than—"

"I know, I know. I just need a reason to let him go. Have to put something in the report, and your vouching for him will do the trick."

"What do we do?"

"We go to the station soon as we're finished. Don't think he wants to spend another night behind bars, do you?"

Eighty-seven

THE JAIL CELL IS NOT AT THE CITY'S JAIL by the curving seawall, the place with the gruesome history that's no longer gruesome because it's topped with a grassy promenade now, where Federico and I've walked on breezy Sunday afternoons. He's far from there.

He's in a holding cell in the back of Ancon Station a few feet from where Harry and I sat talking two hours earlier. Unbelievable.

I huff and pant to keep up with the two men—longer legs than mine. They talk about Federico and how absurd and unjust all this is, yet the way the system works and can't be avoided. That's my Federico they're talking about, and they have no idea. What a whopper of a secret. My heart beats hard as I walk fast and pant.

We climb the steps to the station in the moonlight. The rain has stopped. The air is soft and warm and clean.

The lieutenant greets us. "Good evening."

"Gotta talk to the prisoner," Harry says and breezes by him.

He takes a key from a wooden box on the wall and we go back to the cell and finally . . .

There sits Federico on a cot, reading as though the last thing on his mind is his life being interrupted by accusations of attempted murder. He looks up calmly, a little surprised to see me.

I want to weep, go to him and curl against him, my best friend in the world, the person I love most. It's overpowering, but I don't move. I stand beside Father and watch.

"Mr. Hailey here is going to vouch for you," Harry says, "and I'll be able to write up a release. Shouldn't take more than a few minutes and you'll be out of here."

Harry has respect for Federico. More than anyone except maybe me, he understands him and envies him. It strikes me that the three most important men in my life are standing together in one room—not likely I'll see that again. My face is hot.

I frown, look at the floor.

Father and Harry talk quietly and write out the official report. Federico looks over at me with a slow, lazy smile at all of this—child's play for him. I smile back.

The document is completed. "Now, we'll need your signature," Harry says. "Have to show we've released you."

Federico signs. So does Father. Harry initials on a bottom corner. As Federico turns, he gives me that penetrating curious look, two seconds of it.

What's he thinking?

We move into the front office. Harry gives Federico a train pass and returns several personal articles to him. "Here you go. This'll get you to Peter Miguel. Sorry about this whole thing," he says.

"It's quite all right. Not your fault." Federico shakes Father's hand. "And once again you've been a help," he says. "Thank you." Federico's a gentleman, gracious and calm.

"Well, it never should have happened. Sorry you had to go through it," Father says.

Federico turns to me and makes a quick, courteous bow. He's about to leave and Harry stops him.

"I'm wondering . . . could we get together sometime and talk, maybe on a Sunday? A café somewhere? I'd like to pick your brain about labor practices here, working in the Cut, that sort of thing."

Federico raises his eyebrows with interest. "I'd like that. Any Sunday, then. You know where I live." A little smile between them—the enumerator knows where everybody lives.

Harry's happy and says goodbye.

Federico nods to the three of us, gives us another courteous bow and walks out. Harry takes a deep breath. "Well, I'm looking forward to that."

He puts the paperwork in a filing cabinet, clears the top of his desk, and locks the drawers. The lieutenant says good night to us and we start down the hill.

Harry's feeling good and says, "There's a shooter out there who was so drunk he probably doesn't remember the incident, but at least Malero's not sitting in a jail cell for him. I can sleep better."

"Me, too," says Father.

"I'm going to have a chance to eat with him and talk. I've been wanting to do that for a long time." Harry nods and smiles to himself, no doubt anticipating lunch with the Spaniard.

I'm anticipating a little time with the Spaniard myself.

Eighty-eight

THREE DAYS LATER, ON A SUNDAY, I'm sitting on the porch.

One foot is propped on the railing, the other swings from the edge of the rocker. I'm wearing my nicest white muslin dress, the lady of the house, watching the activity below, fanning my face.

He'll find a way to get us together again. Federico knows how to manage things—I know that now and I trust it. I have only to wait and be available.

Occasionally people pass on the track below: a local woman with two small children carrying a basket of fruit on her head;

an American couple arm in arm; three boys of color with sticks, hitting anything in reach—weeds, rocks, the rails . . .

A figure approaches from the north and grows larger. It's Federico.

I sit up and watch.

He keeps a normal pace as he comes closer, and when he reaches our house, he starts up the steps without hurry or caution, or any sign of concern. He has the same calm as in the holding cell, his cabin, the Tivoli—that quality I've tried to learn from him. The calm of an adult who's seen something of life.

He mounts the steps the same way he did when he came to honor Father, deliberately and with resolve. We finally stand face to face at the screened door.

"I just had lunch with Harry. He tells me you're alone," he says.

"I am, yes. How was lunch?"

He comes into the porch as though he's done it a hundred times and pulls another rocker close to mine and sits.

"Lunch was good. Harry's interesting . . . I like him."

"Me, too."

"Where is your father?"

"You know where he is—making out railroad passes for your compatriots."

"Ah, yes. Why so late in the day?"

"He knows some of the men can't get away until afternoon, so he stays. He says they've earned their leave."

"He's a good man." He puts his hand on my thigh. "Where is your mother?"

"Still in Dayton. How did you know where I was when I went away?"

"I tracked down your father and he told me."

It's peaceful and like I imagined it would be when Mother and Father went to Taboga and we'd have the house to ourselves. He doesn't take his hand off my thigh. We sit awhile longer making small talk, then I lead him inside and we go up to my room. Like a married couple we undress and make love quietly in my bed. We lie there and talk. He's concerned about me, he says, and wants to know how distressed Mother would be if she knew about us.

"Very," I say. "She'd be upset because she doesn't suspect anything like this and she trusts me and she believes a relationship outside of marriage is wrong."

"She was a virgin when she married?"

"Of course. So was Father."

"No." This he doesn't believe.

"Don't you see it in him?"

"Maybe, yes."

"My mother worries that I don't have a boyfriend. She wants me to find someone at school."

"Why don't you?"

That hurts. "Because they're . . . boys. Boys."

A soft smile. "I know," he says. "And if your father knew?"

"He would do whatever Mother tells him to." We lie there naked, a nice breeze across us after the morning rain. "He's not weak, you know—only where Mother is concerned, and it's not exactly weakness. He's just so devoted to her that he does what she wants to please her. He has great qualities."

"I think he does."

"He's thorough."

"That's good, yes." I can tell this is amusing him.

"Last year when he was visiting the building site at the dam he told the workmen to shake the cement bags—they weren't getting everything out. And then when Goethals heard about it he got everyone doing it, and they saved fifty thousand dollars in recovered cement."

"Your father did that?"

"Yes, he did."

"Good for him."

It strikes me I've told him a childish story and I twist my head up to look at him. He still has a half smile so I say it again: "He's not weak at all."

"I didn't say he was and you don't need to apologize for him—he's a good man. He has character, stands up for the workers; he's strong. Weakness is . . . something else—my mother choosing comfort over reality, that's weakness. Your parents are good, honest. I like them."

"The Commission gives Father more responsibility every year, you know—they need people like him."

"They do, yes. They certainly do." He goes quiet, and then he says, "You think the Commission is a fine group of men, do you?"

I look up at him again. "Isn't it?"

"They get away with . . . murder."

"No."

Eighty-nine

THIS IS LIKE OLD TIMES AT THE CABIN. He smiles and tells me all about it.

"You know what they did to get the sand for that cement? You won't read about this in any Commission report."

"What did they do?"

"The sand had to be just right, a very fine consistency, had to be perfect, so they searched around and found it in San Blas—"

"Those little islands?"

"Yes, and they went there and took me along to talk to the Indians. They were going to take the sand no matter what, but they took me along to smooth things over, negotiate if they had to. But the Indians stood there with machetes and said the water and sand are God's gift and they wouldn't sell them to the white man."

"You heard all this?"

"I translated it. They said they'd let us stay overnight but we'd have to be gone by dawn—otherwise they'd kill us." He laughs. "We got out of there."

"The Indians won."

"They thought we were lunatics; I could see it in their eyes. 'Crazy white men'—I didn't bother translating that. I liked seeing the Commission intimidated by men in loincloths with primitive weapons and no big speeches. It's gratifying. Those engineers wanted out of there."

"But they didn't get away with murder."

"They would have tried but they were scared."

"I never heard about that."

"And you won't. Not from any public source. They found the sand they wanted at Nombre de Dios—no locals living there. Nobody to give them a hard time."

"What else haven't I heard about?"

"Plenty of things, all the time. The Commission tells us only what it wants us to know."

I think about this for a while, don't doubt the truth of it, then make what I think is a wise observation.

"But they didn't get away with anything in San Blas."

"Because the engineers didn't want their balls carved off. Have you seen the guns they're putting on Perico and Flamenco? Sixteen inches, the largest weapons the U.S. has now, twenty-mile range, and they're on both islands. Aren't you reading *El Unico* any more? It's all there."

"Yes, I read it, I know all about the guns. Maybe the Spanish Church is right and we shouldn't connect the oceans . . ." I'm trying to be light, make a joke, but he doesn't laugh.

"The oceans have been connected for eons," he says, and he's up on an elbow, his voice raised. "Volcanoes and earthquakes pushed up the Isthmus, that's all. The Church tells us only what it wants us to know, like the Commission—no more, no less."

He's never been angry with me before and I freeze. "I'm sorry," I say.

He realizes how intense he is, takes a minute, then eases back. He exhales and lies still, then pulls me against him; I can feel his heart pounding.

"I'm sorry," he says. "I ruined the week we could have had before, and I don't want to do that again . . . I'm sorry."

"It's all right."

"No, it isn't."

After a while he relaxes and soothes and strokes me, and I lie quiet like a child in his arms.

Some time passes, him stroking me.

Do I know how much I excite him, he says. How often he thinks of me at night or working in the Cut.

He eases himself over me, folding my knees against his shoulders, saying he wants more and more of me.

Downstairs, when he's leaving, he gives me a kiss. A kiss goodbye and a long embrace at the door, just like a married couple, or some kind of couple. That afternoon is the best time we've ever had together. Reunion, sex, talk of things personal and political, a small conflict, resolution, more sex—that's marriage, isn't it? Isn't that what it is? In my embarrassingly sheltered Midwestern brain I think that's it and I'm happy, and the fact that we're a universe apart doesn't matter.

I watch him go down the steps, unhurried and peaceful, and I feel the calm he has. I've got it finally, the real thing. At the bottom near the tracks he looks up, gives me a wave, and walks on, quickly disappearing behind the foliage. I'm so in the moment, I don't want to budge. Not forward. Not backward. The instant is perfect. We're perfect. Don't let anything change.

Father comes home about an hour later and I'm cooking dinner —a baked chicken, a little fryer, actually. Pop it in, take it out in forty-five minutes—easy.

"That smells mighty good," he says coming up the steps, before I can even see his face.

I don't find it necessary to write in my diary that night. I can talk to Federico about the things I'd put on the page.

Ninety

MOTHER IS BACK. She never entirely unpacks and that's unsettling. It indicates how near the end we are and how much she wants to go home for good. It puts a new angle on everything. We're past all the big markers—the locks, the lake, the near impossible cut through Culebra; we're looking at the end. It's in the air.

And because the canal is nearly complete, the Commission is lobbying to keep Americans for ongoing maintenance, the dredging, the increased work of administration when the passage of ships and the real commerce begin. They want Father in the worst way, but he knows it's out of the question and doesn't try to change Mother's mind. He didn't make a deal with her to stay indefinitely, only to the end of construction. He's happy he's had that much.

I let all this go over my head, shut it out. But talk is everywhere, the end is near, and one day I can no longer avoid it. The thought of leaving seizes me and I'm nearly paralyzed.

I'm eighteen, about to graduate, receive a diploma signed by the president of the United States, and it means nothing. I want everything to go on. Time needs to stop. I have what I want now and I can't remember ever feeling so assured or happy or like myself before.

But Oberlin College has accepted me and Mother begins talking about clothes, since everything I have is thin and cool and mostly white, except for jodhpurs and brown leather high-top shoes, which she hopes I'll never put on again. I've long ago outgrown my warm Ohio clothes. I'm more than two inches taller after three years in Panama and I need an entire winter wardrobe. But I don't want to think about clothes or Ohio, and I certainly don't want to accept the fact that canal construction is almost complete. That's when I have to go home.

When Mother talks about college and clothes I nod my head and agree to shopping trips when we're back in Dayton. I try to keep my mind in the present, in Panama, with Federico in the Cut somewhere.

There is no date to sail—it's still months away. The canal is not completed or officially open or filled with water; these are all events yet to come. But resistance to passing time gets a grip on me, and to make it worse, I see Federico less often, sometimes only a few minutes in front of the Tivoli and only twice again in his cabin alone—*only twice*. It's not his fault. Laborers are working longer hours and I have fewer excuses to go out at night. Finally I have none.

Ninety-one

THERE'S AN ACCELERATION OF ACTIVITY and fervor in the Zone, a time of records and groundbreaking events and newsworthy incidents. Thirteen automobiles now cruise the narrow streets of the towns, each registered at one hundred twenty-five dollars, a small fortune to most.

"Not much for a fella rich enough to buy the autocar in the first place," Father observes.

Colonel Goethals starts building macadam roads—a military and tourist necessity, he says.

Mr. Russel from the post office in Ancon hikes across the Isthmus in fourteen hours—a record.

"We could do that, Harry," I say. I'll redirect my anxiety to some physical activity with a goal, challenge myself.

Harry isn't interested. "Second place doesn't count in that kind of thing."

"But just to say we've done it . . ."

"I don't need to say I've done it. I walk everywhere, across whole countries, and fifty miles isn't a challenge. China would be—not the Isthmus."

"You're no fun," I say. He laughs and tells me a flier has come to town. "A flier?" He takes me to meet the pilot.

Mr. Robert G. Fowler shakes my hand, a man with a single-engine hydroplane. He's nice looking, only a little older than Harry and neat as a pin like the Wrights.

"Glad to meet you," I say. "I live next door to the Wrights in Dayton."

"Is that a fact? I was trained at their school, flew on their exhibition team."

"Did you, really? Harry, did you know that?"

"Course I did."

We talk. He's from San Francisco, but he spent time training with Wil and Orville, knows them well, worked with them—small world. He offers to take me up in his plane; he's been barnstorming around Balboa for days. "Have to stir up interest."

I agree. At last I'll fly.

Ninety-two

FOWLER'S MACHINE IS NOTHING LIKE ANYTHING I'VE EVER SEEN. It's called a Gage tractor biplane and sits in the water on floats with an eighty-horsepower Hall-Scott engine, he tells me. Does Orville know about this? I wonder. He must.

I like Fowler. He's a good man with interesting ideas, and much like the boys and Harry, he gets things done.

"My mother's starch box was part of the model for their first wind machine," I boast. "I fetched that box."

Fowler laughs and helps me in. He puts goggles on me. I love it. I'm decked out in jodhpurs again, feeling very much the aviator, and Harry watches from the dock, arms crossed on his chest. For the first time ever I see real concern about my safety on Harry's face; I can see this air travel doesn't appeal to him. For all his being an adventurer, something about flight doesn't sit well with Harry.

People gather—Fowler advertises his flights. A local journalist

for the *Canal Record* will make another of his daily reports on
Fowler's activity:

> Time in the air
> Where to
> With or without a passenger
> Weather
> Reason for descent (usually low fuel)
> And an update: "Still not the right weather conditions
> for Mr. Fowler's historic ocean-to-ocean nonstop flight."

Harry doesn't say a word from the shore as Fowler primes the
engine. It turns over, catches, coughs once, catches again, and
roars, a powerful sound, nothing like the sound of the engine the
boys used ten years earlier. That one did the job but this one lets
you know it means business; lifting this craft is going to be easy
and assured. This is exciting.

Inside the plane behind Fowler, I look out at Harry, who has a
grimace on his face and never takes his eyes off me. Fowler guns
the engine and it roars and whines, and we turn in the water. The
prop wash blows back Harry's hair. He squints, watching us pull
away, then I can't see him anymore.

We're skimming along the water.

A motion-picture camera is at my feet and I shout forward to
Fowler.

"What's the camera for?"

"Belongs to R. E. Duhem. He's gonna photograph the canal
when we make the transcontinental flight."

We're picking up speed. I shout again, can't resist bragging:

"Last year I threw away a dress we made from the Wrights' wing fabric."

"I'd have given you a hundred dollars for it!"

We lift off easy, like a kite, into a quick breeze and a brilliant sun, people looking up at us, shading their eyes, pointing us out for their children. They're suddenly a hundred feet below. We climb light and easy for half a minute longer and start making graceful turns and shallow dips over the bay, everything in miniature below us. We're a soaring bird.

So this is what the boys worked on so long. No wonder they stayed with it—a great sensation, floating, wheeling, climbing, diving. What human being wouldn't want this?

I shout forward, "Let's go see the Cut."

Fowler nods and veers north. A smooth ten-mile cruise along rainforest and canal and there it is, the gully teeming with workers and machines, even more impressive from the sky. Men down there are like ants in a trench and Father's among them somewhere. And Federico. I'm two hundred feet in the air and can't get rid of the obsession.

The men stop working and wave shirts and caps and arms. We circle and tip the wings in response. Another circle and we go back to the bay. A few circles there, a breathtaking dive, a grinding climb, and then Fowler taps a gauge and glances back at me. I lean forward and look: FUEL. EMPTY.

Fowler, unbothered, begins a descent in a wide, smooth circle. He brings us lower until we skim the water and settle lightly onto the surface. We slow and begin pulling toward the dock. The propeller comes to a jerking stop and we glide in.

The crowd's gotten bigger. Fowler grins and waves and helps me out.

"This brings them around," he says.

Ninety-three

Two weeks later. 9:45 a.m.

The Gage hydro-biplane takes off with cameraman and pilot. They head for Culebra, circle, and take moving pictures of the men waving and shovels saluting with puffs of steam. They go north, are rained on over Gamboa, where the motor coughs but comes back, cross Gatun Lake at eighteen hundred feet, then race toward Limon Bay and Cristobal, the fuel gauge on empty. They touch down in a silent, fuelless glide among the rocks off Pier 11.

Fowler's report for the journalists: "The trip was uneventful except for that last bit without gas."

They did it in an hour and thirty-five minutes. Another first and another record set.

None of this makes me feel better.

Ninety-four

MY DIARY IS ONCE AGAIN MY ONLY CONFIDANT, and it fills with pages of everything I feel and do.

Saw Federico a few minutes on the street yesterday after flying—so long without a word from him. He's older and wiser than me and it feels like he's decided to wean us away from each other!!! He's distant but nice, which almost spells it out: we'll be over when the canal is complete. I don't want to think of it. It's a matter of months. I'd rather die.

He told me about seeing a flying machine circling overhead. Did I? Almost didn't believe me when I said I was up there. He gave me that look, the perplexed smile again, trying to figure me out—more mystery in that little Dayton girl than he understands. (That's right!) He mentioned there's more trouble in Spain. Maybe that's why he doesn't contact me more often; maybe weaning doesn't have anything to do with it. I know nothing.

Harry just showed up to take me to Colonel Goethals's court. For three years I've been asking to go and now that I've lost interest, he appears at the door. Oh well.

"I'm so glad you're going to see it," says Mother. "Another Zone experience before it ends, and I want to hear all about it."

Goethals's patriarchal Sunday court, foolish to miss it after being here so long. And it will be a major distraction.

Harry and I hop the train to Ancon early. The court will end around noon. By then the colonel will have seen a hundred people with their various grievances and, acting as both judge and jury, will have made a hundred decisions. I've heard about it since we got here. Few will complain they've been denied justice. Forty thousand workers speaking forty-five different languages, and they all know the colonel's office door is open to them on Sunday morning.

I'm not going to think about Federico. I'll just ride along with Harry and keep my mind on what I'm about to see.

Ninety-five

MIDMORNING WE CLIMB THE THOUSAND STEPS of the administration building. Beside us the line of waiting workers snakes out the front. Goethals's big office is on the right in a wide hallway hung with maps and blueprints, and there they stand, men and women of every color, speaking dozens of languages, some with children in hand, all patient, all reasonably quiet though every sound echoes.

We keep walking and Harry leads me past the line and directly into the office; he's been there many times in his capacity as policeman/enumerator/interpreter. He finds a spot inside the door where we can observe.

The room is hot, insufferably hot. Tall windows on one side are open but the air is still—there's not a breath of movement. I feel irritable but I know I feel no more heat than everyone else, so I stand quietly and endure it.

Goethals in his customary white suit sits solemnly behind his desk and listens to each worker present his grievance. Then, after a short consideration, he hands down justice—efficient, dependable, undisputed. It's pretty amazing, and gradually I forget the heat and lose myself in watching the process.

A wife has marital woes, which are quickly dispensed— Goethals handles civil as well as minor criminal matters.

The social-committee chairman sets a date for a Tivoli ballroom dance and Goethals gives the okay.

Harsh treatment by a foreman is resolved.

Failure to get a promotion is taken care of.

A request for special privileges is denied and another is granted.

Then a builder steps up and the rhythm changes. This man has attitude. You can see it in the way he stands and speaks. He takes himself seriously, above these petty domestic disputes and social arrangements, and he makes that clear to the colonel.

"I cannot possibly complete the pump house in the time allotted," he says with authority.

"What time would that be?" Goethals says.

"The time in your letter, sir."

"I don't recall the letter."

"A letter about the work in Miraflores." The builder produces the letter—he's ready for this.

The secretary gives the letter to the colonel, who glances at it, then looks up.

"This is not a letter. This is an order."

The builder blinks. "Sir . . . ?"

"It's a deadline. Get it done," he says. "Do you want to talk about anything else?"

The builder stammers, "N-n-o," and the secretary touches his arm to make him move aside. He's stupefied.

Next case.

Can't help liking Goethals.

Ninety-six

IT MOVES FAST AND I KEEP MY MIND ON THE PROCEEDINGS—the various human appeals, the deferential complainers, the colonel himself, so assured through all of it. I like this, the way it's done and the justice. I wonder if Federico's been here. He'd like it and Harry clearly loves it.

Two more complaints resolved, then Harry leans toward me and whispers, "Here—this is what we came to see."

It's a shovel engineer, and he tells Goethals he's been discharged unjustly. Harry straightens and tilts his head to see Goethals's face more closely.

"What was the reason for your discharge?" the colonel says.

"Because I can't play baseball."

"That's the reason?"

"Yes, sir." Harry nudges me. "They've hired another shovel operator with a better pitching arm, sir."

There's a half smile on Harry's face as his eyes flick from the colonel to the shoveler and back to the colonel. Goethals hesitates a moment longer than usual, then speaks. "They want shovelers on the Pacific end. Report in the morning for work." The colonel turns to his secretary. "Ring them up; arrange it."

The shoveler steps over to the secretary and they begin taking care of the matter. Harry nudges me again, smiling. "Let's go."

In the hall where we can talk, Harry's still grinning.

"They've got their pitcher and the shovel man's got his job . . . You've got to hand it to the old man. Course, he had to do that. He's the one pushing for baseball, says it's a morale builder, but he can't condone an unjust firing—he can't let that happen." He shakes his head in admiration. "He took care of it."

"I didn't know you were interested in baseball, Harry."

"It's the justice I'm interested in. Well, I'm playing short-stop . . ." He gives me a wink and suddenly stops walking. "Malero!"

I look up. Federico is standing in line.

Harry pumps his hand and smiles. "It's good to see you."

"Nice to see you again, Harry."

I smile at Federico; my chest tightens.

"Why are you here?" Harry asks him.

"It's nothing much. I've been on the wrong pay scale since I came back to work after being sick—a clerical error, but it still isn't corrected."

Harry waves it off. "He'll take care of it in seconds. I didn't know you were sick."

"Months ago. I'm fine now." Then, to me as though we are simply acquaintances, "How is your father?"

"Very well, working hard."

"Thank him for me again, will you?"

"Yes, I will."

Two workers push us from behind, wanting to get by, and the line moves Federico ahead. We're separated.

"Good luck," Harry calls back to him.

Federico nods and is gone.

Our shoes click on the hall floor. Harry muses. "He's a mystery . . ." We're working our way through the crowd. "Hard to know. He's political, we think along the same lines, but . . . something else is there—I don't know what it is. And you can't get close to him—he keeps his distance. There's something . . . inscrutable about him." Then, after a moment, "You'd have to know him to see it."

"Of course."

We emerge into brilliant sunlight.

"Shortstop, huh?" I say.

Harry grins, forgets Federico. "I'm pretty good," he says.

On the train we chat and I look out the window trying to actually see what is passing, but inside I am roiling and later can't remember what Harry and I talked about, though we laughed a few times.

In my diary that night I add to my Goethals's court account: *I'm willing to sleep, but I'm not willing to wake up. That's just asking too much. Teenage angst, no doubt—a word I've learned from Dr. Freud by way of Federico.*

Ninety-seven

THIS ANGST IS GETTING WORSE—bigger, darker, more unescapable. It doesn't help that there's a sense of heightened excitement in the air. The men take increasing pride in the work they're completing; people now talk about the end, who's staying on and who's leaving and where they're going, et cetera. Goethals tells journalists about the great accomplishment and how people are fired up to be near the end. It's a common topic of conversation: *the final days are on us.* But it's the end for me, and I use the word *cataclysmic* in my diary because I'm in a dramatic state of mind and having painful and disturbing dreams.

Men are reporting to work early and staying late without overtime—mostly the American work force. The workers of color continue as always with their daily backbreaking labor, only vaguely aware of the accomplishment.

On May 20, 1913, I make note that two shovels digging toward each other in Culebra narrow the gap all day long, digging and shoveling like mad, and people gather to watch when they hear what's happening. In the afternoon the shovels stand nose to nose and all hell breaks loose. Whistles hoot for miles along the Cut, the noise heard all over the Zone.

I read about it in the *Canal Record* because it's too painful to watch, and hearing talk about it in our house is more than enough.

The Cut is as deep as it will go—forty feet above sea level, the locks handling the difference—and now it goes all the way through, ocean to ocean.

Much is made of this at school—it's our last two weeks, with graduation and summer break coming up. Alice Kirk, daughter of shovel man Joseph Kirk, driver of shovel No. 222, is instructed to write the names of the shovel drivers on the board: her own father's and that of D. J. MacDonal, shovel No. 230.

"Remember those names," says Mrs. Ewing, more than aware that history is being made.

Eleven days later we're instructed to write about more history: the upper gates at Gatun are complete and function perfectly. Father reads aloud from the *Canal Record:* ". . . the gates swung to a position halfway open, then shut, opened again wide, closed completely, all noiselessly, without jar or vibration, at all times under perfect control." He looks up, beaming. I try to smile back.

It's another accomplishment moving the whole monstrous project toward its final day, and I have to excuse myself and go upstairs.

Like the girls I scorned at school whispering about their boy-friends, in a constant fever of romance and heightened emotion, I collapse on my bed and weep, sobbing and choking. I can't change what's happening. I can't change Federico and his life or mine or Colonel Goethals's damned unstoppable, unflappable leadership toward the great Yankee achievement, breaking the back of the Divide. The canal is going to be complete. And soon. What nature did to thwart the work has had no effect. The slides continue but so does the dredging, and Goethals orders it to continue as long as necessary, forever if need be. He'll match nature with endurance and he'll beat her. What do I do about that?

I understand it for the first time and I accept it that evening, beaten, like nature, my heart breaking. Like a child who's lost a parent, I weep secretly and inconsolably. There's no one to talk to about it, only Federico, who's the source of the pain and my most intimate friend and confidant. What would I say to him? Not something silly like "Will you write?" Or "Let me come with you." Dime-novel stuff.

But I want to say *something*—beg him to keep in touch with me, send Spanish newspapers because I'll never find *El Unico* in Oberlin, tell me what he's doing, how the rebellion's going, something, anything. I'll have no real information unless war breaks out—only that will make it to our Midwestern papers.

What if I arrange to come to Spain to study? There's an idea. But he'll be busy fomenting rebellion. Maybe we could meet somewhere else—London, Paris, even . . . Am I likely to get to those places? Could he take time off from fomenting to visit me?

After sobbing on my bed and running through a list of alternatives, I pull myself together, wash my face, and go back downstairs. Harry's come by. He's talking about a rescue expedition he's going on the next day. The lake is rising and some of the indigenous Panamanians are too stubborn to leave. I want to see this and it'll keep me busy.

"Can I come along?"

Ninety-eight

I'M IN JODHPURS AGAIN, this time in Harry's thirty-foot Zone police launch, American and Panamanian flags flying fore and aft, a canvas canopy supported by four poles over our heads.

An unimpressive gasoline motor pushes us across the unbroken expanse of rising Gatun Lake, moving us through the top of the submerged forest, an otherworldly scene. No matter how I feel, I will not waste my last days in Panama. I will see this unnatural event—make myself see it. Something grim and hard is forming in me. Reality, maybe?

The top of the jungle under us—the tips of trees—rises out of the lake. Royal palms stand up to their necks in water; corpulent century-old giants of the jungle on tiptoe with their jagged noses just above the surface, gasping their last.

Mango trees laden with fruit are descending into the flood. The lake is so mirrorlike that we can see the drowning palms and blue sky as plainly above the surface as on it.

A protruding stump of palm looks like a piece double its length, a water thermometer.

An angle of wood floats at exactly the same angle in perfect distortion.

We cruise through this strange waterscape in silence.

"What's the matter?" Harry asks me. He's pretty somber himself, but I'm unusually quiet.

"I'm sad to be leaving," I say, blurting out to Harry what I can't say to Federico because I'm afraid of upsetting some invisible balance between us.

"You're leaving? I thought there was another year's work after it opens."

"The Commission wants us to stay, but Mother wants to get back and I'm going to college."

"Ah," he says.

I look at him hard. Something's different with him. He's disturbed and quiet.

We putt across the glassy lake a few minutes longer, then he says, "You've been like family to me, you know."

There's a deep feeling in his voice I've never heard before, but I can tell it's not about me or my family.

"We won't go for a few more weeks . . . end of summer, for certain. Father may stay on a little while."

He nods and looks out over the glassy surface.

"You'll come see us," I say.

"I won't be in the neighborhood, I don't think . . ." He means Dayton. His plans are worldwide, a bitter joke.

He'll be off in some other country on a new adventure, but he has an uncharacteristic, angry look on his face and I know my gloomy mood hasn't brought that on. I'm about to ask what's bothering him when a snow-white slender heron rises from the water as we bear down on him, and then we're suddenly surrounded by acres of big codlike fish floating dead on the surface among branches and forest rubbish.

"Rising water has spread some poisonous mineral from the soil. It's killing everything," Harry says.

We pass a jungle family on their way to market in their *cayucas* laden with mounds of produce—mangoes, bananas, plantains— and a duck and a chicken tied by a leg standing on top. They gaze complacently at the scene with the air of experienced tourists. I envy them. I want their cocky oblivion.

Ninety-nine

WE PUTT TOWARD A MOUND OF LAND STILL ABOVE WATER and a solitary old native sitting on a knoll near his thatched shelter.

"He took to the bush when he heard the lake was rising," Harry says. "He refuses to leave."

"Does he have to?"

"He's on U.S. public domain."

I snort with contempt—the absurdity of public domain to a man rooted for centuries in this land. Harry shoots me a warning glance—the old man might not know I'm on his side. But the old man's face is passive.

We pull the launch onto the grass and walk toward him, Harry speaking in some skilled mix of Spanish and Indian dialect. They understand each other. Once more Harry amazes me.

The old fellow barely nods, holding a bundle in his arms. Harry knows he has to move quickly—there are others he has to save—but he takes a minute anyway. He looks around, finds a stick, and pounds a mango tree till it drops most of its fruit, and he does the same with red *maranones* and fills a basket lying abandoned by the shelter. Harry puts the basket in the launch for the old man, then helps him in. The man sits, not once putting his eyes on me. He watches mournfully as Harry touches a match to the thatched roof of his home, comes back to the launch, and shoves us off.

In minutes the roof is pouring a column of smoke straight up into the air. Even the old man's table and chair and barrel of odds and ends outside the hut catch fire. We move away and start across the lake, losing sight of the knoll, but the blazing four poles that supported the roof can be seen against the sky.

Whole villages have been burned in the lake territory, owners paid condemnation damages by the *yanquis* in plenty of time to leave, but some don't, like this old fellow, who shows no emotion at his loss.

We're soon caught in the top branches of a tree.

Harry and I work up a sweat poling the boat free, pushing against submerged limbs, twisting, grunting. The old man hardly raises his eyes to watch our struggle. Finally free, Harry pulls the gas motor into action and we deliver the old man with his bundle and basket of fruit to safe ground. Several people there are passing on their way to market and he joins them. A small boy quickly takes charge of the basket, seeing a little profit for himself if he puts in an effort.

We move out again and little thatched cottages begin to appear on knolls along the way, the inhabitants waiting to be boated to safety. This is higher land, so the lower branches of the trees stand out of the water, though a death sentence is on them, too.

"In the deepest parts, there's a forest larger than ten Fontainebleaus already submerged," Harry says. "Lake's rising two inches a day and the colonel guarantees an eighty-seven-foot level. A hundred and sixty-five square miles of lush green will disappear forever. In the future—way in the future—men'll dive down and take a look at the sunken cities. They're older than Pizarro, you know, so they'll really be ancient by then. They'll want to see what it was like. Antiquity."

One Hundred

WE MOTOR SEVERAL FAMILIES TO HIGHER LAND, some with possessions, some empty-handed—our contribution to the complete removal of their lives by encroaching empire and world trade. Harry does his work—firm and helpful, but he doesn't like it. One by one we take the indigenous inhabitants to safety, stopping only a few minutes to drift and eat sandwiches, then we're on our way again. The transporting continues until it's late and time to start back.

"It'll get dark fast," Harry says and turns the launch.

Within minutes two raging showers pass over us, moving discs of pelting rain like the shadow of the sun in an eclipse.

We encounter several flocks of little birds in the tops of trees, sitting at rest, watching the late afternoon.

"They're not far from land—what's the matter with them?" Harry says. He pulls out an army rifle that could kill an elephant and blasts into the sky. Echoes roll across the silent, flooded world and the birds scatter and fly landward. The echoes fade.

We motor on and Harry is sullen, pondering. I'm consumed with my own problems. Finally he speaks.

"A bunch of foreigners show up, say they're turning your

Harry shoots me a hard look and shakes his head, doesn't want to talk about it.

I go quiet. But I wonder if they argued about that. About cutting it off clean before she leaves. Did Harry want to carry on to the end? He must have, to the last final night. Which of them didn't want that, I wonder. Harry or her?

"I'm sorry," I say.

"It's all right." His voice is gravelly.

But he won't be holding her in his arms again. She's gone. And will he find what he had with her in the next country he tramps off to? Will he find the sexual camaraderie? I know what that is and how addicting. She has the look in her eye, the quiet, crooked smile. They had it, all right, and now it's gone for good. "Maybe you'll change your mind and—"

"Don't start again," he says, and that really does end it.

He breathes deep, lifts his chin, and looks around. "Where's that train? You can set your watch by this railroad—" and the engine comes into view.

I check my watch. Exactly on time.

One Hundred and Two

DIARY, TWO WEEKS LATER: *The last of the spillway gates is closed at Gatun Dam. The lake has reached a depth of forty-eight feet and is rising to its full height.*

A few days after that Federico approaches me near the Tivoli.

He's wearing the white suit and cuts a swath through the world into a lake, going to float steamers over you. You've never heard of steamers, don't need them, but sure enough one day we come snorting down on you in a motorboat as you're lying under the thatch roof your grandfather built. We tell you to get out of here, we're going to burn your house, going to make a lake, right over these banana trees you played under and that *ciega* tree your mother got married under and this jungle path you've been courting your girl on—it's all going to disappear, come on. We give them a bag of metal disks and they want to know what they are. That's money, brother, coinage, lucre, good anywhere in the world . . . Better get used to it." Harry steers straight toward the dam, his voice even and angry.

"Always picked what you ate from trees and used the same tree to build shelter? Never mind. Take these coins, buy a farm that's bigger, better, above the water line. From there you can watch the only world you've ever known sink under a rising lake." He turns to me. "How do you buy a farm and exchange pieces of metal for food when you've always knocked food out of a mango tree, the one behind your grandfather's house? How do you do that?" He turns back to the lake slipping by us.

I have no answer and he doesn't expect one.

He motors on, frowning and silent, toward the bulk of Gatun locks rising on the horizon. In a few minutes we dock the launch and I stay close to him; he knows where we're going.

We hurry across the locks and dam to the marshland beyond the spillway, where he makes inquiries about an attempt to burn the I.C.C. launch attached to dredge number something-or-other—police business. It's beginning to get dark. I want to go home.

WE STAND WAITING FOR OUR TRAIN AT THE STATION and I'm shaking, though it's sultry hot. Harry notices.

"Do you have a chill?"

"No, no. Just . . . the flooding and what it's doing to the people bothers me. The way it does you."

"Mmm," he says. But there's something more upsetting him than displaced Indians.

"What's wrong, Harry? You look terrible."

No answer, then finally: "I feel terrible," he says. "Mrs. McManus . . ."

Mrs. McManus. I've forgotten her. I've been so obsessed with my own love life—can I call it that? Harry has one, too, and I never thought to ask about it.

"Will Ruby be staying with you?"

He looks at me, shocked; I've called her by her first name. It feels natural, and giving her a title seems silly. I'm in his grown-up world now, whether he knows it or not. "Is she a wanderer, too?" I say.

"'Fraid not."

"Ah. That's the problem?"

"Not anymore. She's going home next week. Back to Nebraska."

He's been stabbed. I know all about that, and that is the weary anger in his eyes. He's been chewing on it all day, and the plight of native Panamanians has made it worse.

"Her father offered to set me up in the family business, tak[ ] me in, make me a partner," he says.

"What does he do?"

"Winter wheat. They're filthy rich, I gather. God only know[ ] what she's written to them about me—probably sent pictures, [ ] don't know what else. She may have built me up way too much[ ]"

"She wouldn't need to do that about you, Harry. It sounds li[ ] a great offer."

"Not if you're a wanderer." He's torn, I can see it. "It's death [ ] settle down. For me it is. Freedom or death, that's my choice."

"She won't travel with you?"

He shakes his head, looks off. "You can't blame her. She wan[ ] a family, some kind of security. She wants to have a home, kid[ ] She's already lost a husband . . ." A crack in his voice.

"So it's ended? You've split up?"

"Yep. Said our goodbyes. All over." He straightens, strong a[ ] manly again.

We stand there, the train not pulling in yet, a few aimle[ ] people milling around. He goes on, can't let it go now that I'[ ] opened the wound.

"I avoid any place I think she might be. She does the same f[ ] me . . . Trying to keep it painless. Only way I know to do it." [ ] takes a deep breath, looks down the track, checks his watch.

What a pair we are—lovelorn grievers. We think we're abo[ ] all the misery, footloose and fancy-free, but we take the tumb[ ] plenty hard. I'll never scoff at heartbreak again.

"Why not keep seeing her until she leaves?" I say. "It's the l[ ] time you'll have together."

crowd like a visiting dignitary—men look, women stare. He is so absorbed in his thoughts, he doesn't notice.

"I've earned a day off," he says. It's a weekday.

I've graduated. I'm out of school.

We sit on the bench where we first met. (This registers with me—I wonder if it does with him.)

"I suppose you'll be leaving soon," he says.

So it begins. Officially. The gentle cutting free.

He's going to tie it up for us, end it with minimal hurt feelings. He's even dressed for the occasion.

I ready myself, can't believe this is happening—him making it official.

"Yes," I say. "In a few weeks. After the opening." My voice doesn't crack. I'm no little girl anymore.

But I want to grab him by the perfect white shirt and shake him. I want to disturb that calm I've envied for so long and make him talk, really talk to me, about himself and the mess in Spain and how it affects him, what it does to him all day and night and how it twists his gut and heart and every feeling part of him, and how I make it easier, even a little easier, just being there. I don't want his theories or his history or to see brief slices of his life and pain. I want all of him. But I stay calm. And I keep my voice even, the way he likes. I am his good girl, his American tomboy with whom he's had so much pleasure and so little trouble. I won't change that—I don't have that much courage.

So we talk. And it's proper and quiet:

"Yes, I look forward to college."

"You'll do well."

"I suppose so."

"I'm sure of it—you're very bright."

"How about you? Will you continue working?"

"For a while, another few months."

"More pick and shovel?"

"Yes. In different places . . ."

No sexual camaraderie, just the pleasant conversation of recently introduced tourists. In a matter of minutes he's changed us from lovers to friends and I'm shaken, even though I saw it coming.

I wonder if it shows, if I'm pale.

He's skilled at this sort of thing, controlling a crowd; he can certainly control me. No wonder he's the leader of the rebels. He can stir emotions and bring them to a fevered pitch or neutralize them, whichever he wants. He's just neutralized me. There's not another word about matters in Spain or ideals, nothing the least bit intimate, nothing about books—can't go there. A few innocuous words about school: Will I miss my friends? When was graduation? Standard fare. Pleasantries.

Let me slap the politeness off that face, please. I am so angry and hurt. We're in an emotionally charged cocoon and he's cutting with a sharp knife, skillfully, trying to keep it painless—the bastard. Be rotten to me, Federico—make it easier.

"Come," he says. "We have to see this." And he walks me to the edge of the Cut, no hand holding, no touching. (That's over, too?) "Look."

My brain is fogged, my throat gripped and squeezed tight. I stand there blank and do as he says. I watch.

world into a lake, going to float steamers over you. You've never heard of steamers, don't need them, but sure enough one day we come snorting down on you in a motorboat as you're lying under the thatch roof your grandfather built. We tell you to get out of here, we're going to burn your house, going to make a lake, right over these banana trees you played under and that *ciega* tree your mother got married under and this jungle path you've been courting your girl on—it's all going to disappear, come on. We give them a bag of metal disks and they want to know what they are. That's money, brother, coinage, lucre, good anywhere in the world . . . Better get used to it." Harry steers straight toward the dam, his voice even and angry.

"Always picked what you ate from trees and used the same tree to build shelter? Never mind. Take these coins, buy a farm that's bigger, better, above the water line. From there you can watch the only world you've ever known sink under a rising lake." He turns to me. "How do you buy a farm and exchange pieces of metal for food when you've always knocked food out of a mango tree, the one behind your grandfather's house? How do you do that?" He turns back to the lake slipping by us.

I have no answer and he doesn't expect one.

He motors on, frowning and silent, toward the bulk of Gatun locks rising on the horizon. In a few minutes we dock the launch and I stay close to him; he knows where we're going.

We hurry across the locks and dam to the marshland beyond the spillway, where he makes inquiries about an attempt to burn the I.C.C. launch attached to dredge number something-or-other— police business. It's beginning to get dark. I want to go home.

One Hundred and One

WE STAND WAITING FOR OUR TRAIN AT THE STATION and I'm shaking, though it's sultry hot. Harry notices.

"Do you have a chill?"

"No, no. Just . . . the flooding and what it's doing to the people bothers me. The way it does you."

"Mmm," he says. But there's something more upsetting him than displaced Indians.

"What's wrong, Harry? You look terrible."

No answer, then finally: "I feel terrible," he says. "Mrs. McManus . . ."

Mrs. McManus. I've forgotten her. I've been so obsessed with my own love life—can I call it that? Harry has one, too, and I never thought to ask about it.

"Will Ruby be staying with you?"

He looks at me, shocked; I've called her by her first name. It feels natural, and giving her a title seems silly. I'm in his grownup world now, whether he knows it or not. "Is she a wanderer, too?" I say.

"'Fraid not."

"Ah. That's the problem?"

"Not anymore. She's going home next week. Back to Nebraska."

He's been stabbed. I know all about that, and that is the weary anger in his eyes. He's been chewing on it all day, and the plight of native Panamanians has made it worse.

"Her father offered to set me up in the family business, take me in, make me a partner," he says.

"What does he do?"

"Winter wheat. They're filthy rich, I gather. God only knows what she's written to them about me—probably sent pictures, I don't know what else. She may have built me up way too much."

"She wouldn't need to do that about you, Harry. It sounds like a great offer."

"Not if you're a wanderer." He's torn, I can see it. "It's death to settle down. For me it is. Freedom or death, that's my choice."

"She won't travel with you?"

He shakes his head, looks off. "You can't blame her. She wants a family, some kind of security. She wants to have a home, kids. She's already lost a husband . . ." A crack in his voice.

"So it's ended? You've split up?"

"Yep. Said our goodbyes. All over." He straightens, strong and manly again.

We stand there, the train not pulling in yet, a few aimless people milling around. He goes on, can't let it go now that I've opened the wound.

"I avoid any place I think she might be. She does the same for me . . . Trying to keep it painless. Only way I know to do it." He takes a deep breath, looks down the track, checks his watch.

What a pair we are—lovelorn grievers. We think we're above all the misery, footloose and fancy-free, but we take the tumble plenty hard. I'll never scoff at heartbreak again.

"Why not keep seeing her until she leaves?" I say. "It's the last time you'll have together."

Harry shoots me a hard look and shakes his head, doesn't want to talk about it.

I go quiet. But I wonder if they argued about that. About cutting it off clean before she leaves. Did Harry want to carry on to the end? He must have, to the last final night. Which of them didn't want that, I wonder. Harry or her?

"I'm sorry," I say.

"It's all right." His voice is gravelly.

But he won't be holding her in his arms again. She's gone. And will he find what he had with her in the next country he tramps off to? Will he find the sexual camaraderie? I know what that is and how addicting. She has the look in her eye, the quiet, crooked smile. They had it, all right, and now it's gone for good. "Maybe you'll change your mind and—"

"Don't start again," he says, and that really does end it.

He breathes deep, lifts his chin, and looks around. "Where's that train? You can set your watch by this railroad—" and the engine comes into view.

I check my watch. Exactly on time.

One Hundred and Two

DIARY, TWO WEEKS LATER: *The last of the spillway gates is closed at Gatun Dam. The lake has reached a depth of forty-eight feet and is rising to its full height.*

A few days after that Federico approaches me near the Tivoli. He's wearing the white suit and cuts a swath through the crowd like a visiting dignitary—men look, women stare. He is so absorbed in his thoughts, he doesn't notice.

"I've earned a day off," he says. It's a weekday.

I've graduated. I'm out of school.

We sit on the bench where we first met. (This registers with me—I wonder if it does with him.)

"I suppose you'll be leaving soon," he says.

So it begins. Officially. The gentle cutting free.

He's going to tie it up for us, end it with minimal hurt feelings. He's even dressed for the occasion.

I ready myself, can't believe this is happening—him making it official.

"Yes," I say. "In a few weeks. After the opening." My voice doesn't crack. I'm no little girl anymore.

But I want to grab him by the perfect white shirt and shake him. I want to disturb that calm I've envied for so long and make him talk, really talk to me, about himself and the mess in Spain and how it affects him, what it does to him all day and night and how it twists his gut and heart and every feeling part of him, and how I make it easier, even a little easier, just being there. I don't want his theories or his history or to see brief slices of his life and pain. I want all of him. But I stay calm. And I keep my voice even, the way he likes. I am his good girl, his American tomboy with whom he's had so much pleasure and so little trouble. I won't change that—I don't have that much courage.

So we talk. And it's proper and quiet:

"Yes, I look forward to college."

"You'll do well."

"I suppose so."

"I'm sure of it—you're very bright."

"How about you? Will you continue working?"

"For a while, another few months."

"More pick and shovel?"

"Yes. In different places . . ."

No sexual camaraderie, just the pleasant conversation of recently introduced tourists. In a matter of minutes he's changed us from lovers to friends and I'm shaken, even though I saw it coming.

I wonder if it shows, if I'm pale.

He's skilled at this sort of thing, controlling a crowd; he can certainly control me. No wonder he's the leader of the rebels. He can stir emotions and bring them to a fevered pitch or neutralize them, whichever he wants. He's just neutralized me. There's not another word about matters in Spain or ideals, nothing the least bit intimate, nothing about books—can't go there. A few innocuous words about school: Will I miss my friends? When was graduation? Standard fare. Pleasantries.

Let me slap the politeness off that face, please. I am so angry and hurt. We're in an emotionally charged cocoon and he's cutting with a sharp knife, skillfully, trying to keep it painless—the bastard. Be rotten to me, Federico—make it easier.

"Come," he says. "We have to see this." And he walks me to the edge of the Cut, no hand holding, no touching. (That's over, too?) "Look."

My brain is fogged, my throat gripped and squeezed tight. I stand there blank and do as he says. I watch.

One Hundred and Three

PHOTOGRAPHERS CARRY THEIR GEAR INTO THE WORK AREA.
Journalists follow. This is big news for the hometown papers.
But I'm a zombie now.

A steam shovel lifts out the last load of rock, dumps it onto locomotive No. 260, and it's hauled away to applause. Work crews
move in. They begin tearing up the last of the track, the steam
shovel pulling at the rails like they're obstinate bailing wire. The
job is done in less than half an hour.

Cameras click on either side of us. Father is down there somewhere, but I can't bring myself to search for him. Photographers
move back and forth angling for the best shots; journalists urge
comments from workers to spice the articles they'll wire back
that evening. Their shirts streaked with sweat, mud caked to
their shoes and pant legs—once in a lifetime, all of this. To me it
looks like it's happening on a movie screen.

The clearing ends and the journalists and photographers
climb out. The crowd begins to break up and a thick, uneasy
silence falls between Federico and me.

"That will be in papers tomorrow," I say, my voice surpris-
ingly solid.

"Big headlines in the States?"

"I'm sure it will be."

Here's where I begin thinking it through: *I started it, didn't
I? Conniving, plotting, scheming, out at night, running all over the
place to get to him. I did it. He came along only for the ride—he's*

innocent. And now it's over and he's ending it like a gentleman. I should be grateful for that. The logic begins to overcome the lunacy and I see his lips moving.

"Let's walk awhile," he says.

We do.

I make no effort to be chatty. I want to hate him but I can't, not unless I stay completely insane and I don't. My mind clears and I begin to feel suffocated.

Children scoot by us, mostly American, and tourists bump and jostle. A band plays off somewhere.

Straight ahead of me, approaching through the crowd, is Mother.

One Hundred and Four

SHE WALKS TOWARD US and will have to pass close, though she hasn't seen us yet. Then she does. She smiles broadly.

"Did I miss it?" she says. Her eyes are on Federico.

"I'm afraid so. Everything's cleared out," I say. "Federico, my mother." I don't know whether to introduce her using her first name or as Mrs. Hailey, and I fumble. Finally Mother saves me when she summons the most social grace I've ever seen from her:

"Louisa," she says and shakes Federico's hand. "I'm so pleased to meet you. I remember when you came to our house and all of you sang."

"Yes, yes. Pleased to make your acquaintance," he says with a hint of that bow.

Smashing. She loves it. "Did you see everything?"

"We did, yes. Very impressive."

Approval is written all over Mother's face. She likes him (the pin-perfect white suit, the British accent). And she takes him for exactly what he is, a well-educated young man, but mistakenly thinks he's in a position of authority—if not with the Commission, then with a bank, or a government institution, or a large business seeking expansion in the Zone. Not a worker. In her mind he must have been leading the workers that day in some special capacity.

As usual Federico is unperturbed and in his courtly manner says, "Will you both join me for supper?"

That will take a chunk out of the money he can send home— a couple of weeks' pay or more, I'm sure. But before I can say anything Mother speaks up. "That's very nice but I'm afraid my husband is expecting me. You two go on without me."

She's graceful in declining but it's obvious she wants us to be alone. She says goodbye and moves on.

We walk on quietly for a minute.

"I'm glad you met her," I say.

"She's very nice."

Federico says nothing more about her in spite of all our discussions about parents and the danger of being discovered. There's nothing to discover anymore.

We eat at a small street café. I'm drained and enjoy the simple good food and superficial talk about the fellow running the place, an East Indian with hopes of going back to Delhi to finish his law studies, a typical Panamanian story. Nothing more about inequity in the Zone or anywhere else. That's personal and passionate and that's over.

It's dark when we finish and we join other Zoners to watch the piles of old ties from Father's railroad tracks burn, the climax of the day's events.

"Up in flames," Federico says.

The bonfires snake up the canal for miles, lighting the night. Next to us a *New York Times* correspondent is taking notes for the cable he'll send. He reads it out to the crowd: "A reduction of nine thousand men in the work force. Ninety-seven million cubic yards of material removed to make the canal. Firelight stretching up the length of the channel as far as the eye can see . . ."

History's being made, for sure. He hasn't exaggerated and it's impressive. The fires leap and light Federico's face, and the moment grips me. I can't help myself. I lean against him and he puts his arm around me and holds me like an old friend, an old lover, knowing what I feel.

We watch the bonfires, our faces ruddy in the glow, the smell of dirt and creosote in the starry night. And when it's over, the fires burned out, he delivers me back home.

WE'LL ALWAYS HAVE PANAMA
One Hundred and Five

WE'LL SEE THE FINAL CANAL EVENTS TOGETHER. We actually plan it. We'll make small formal occasions of them, try to enjoy ourselves.

It's what he wants, this courteous, civil separation so that it's a reasonably tolerable memory for me, for both of us.

Actually, I hate it, the elaborate arrangement so I'll become accustomed to seeing him as "Harry's friend," Mother approving of him, all aboveboard, a public friendship. Does he think this will erase everything else?

Now who's naive?

For the lockage event in Gatun we're together again, and I do begin getting used to it—or I'm getting used to misery.

We meet at about ten in the morning and find a spot in the crowd of people, several thousand clustered at the rim of the lock walls. We stand pressed together by the pack of observers and watch a sturdy seagoing tug, the *Gatun,* used for hauling mud barges in the Atlantic entrance, come plowing down toward us in the morning sunshine. I'm happy enough just to be with Federico. The tug is cleaned up and decorated with flags, ready to be the first vessel raised to the level of the lake.

Men lean on the handrails on top of the closed lock gates.

Colonel Goethals, in shirtsleeves with a furled umbrella, moves from point to point on top of a lock wall to see the proceedings at a perfect angle.

A photographer stands suspended in a huge cement bucket from the cableway, his camera on a tripod aimed at the action, waiting for things to begin.

Federico and I stand pressed against the rim of the wall, under my white parasol—Federico told me I'd need it. I know he likes the look of me holding it. I still dress to please him.

Twice school friends pass and I introduce him as a friend of the family. They're impressed and go off whispering and giggling.

"They seem nice enough," he says.

Don't try to foist them off on me to take your place, Federico. This is hard enough.

Then everything begins.

The mob squeezes forward and we're pushed together even more.

The valves are opened to fill the upper chamber, and instead of gasps of awe there's a wave of little cries.

One Hundred and Six

To everyone's surprise the swirling caramel water contains frogs.

This triggers laughter and exclamations and clicking Kodaks, although the rushing movement of water couldn't possibly allow a clear shot of tumbling frogs, jumbled together as they are, legs outstretched, flailing, thrashing. Years of building and planning and importance attached to that moment, and the frogs steal the show.

But the bosses don't mind. They laugh, too, and the upper lock fills as it's meant to, not a single hitch in the whole maneuver.

Federico and I watch, mildly amused—pretty dull compared to our sultry afternoons in his cabin, food and talk and coupling everywhere, the slightly urgent awareness that Augusto will be walking in at any minute. Time is speeding us further away from those erotic hours.

But at the moment, the crowd presses us together. There's nothing we can do about it. The feel of him is unbearably sensual to me. It must be to him, too. He looks away and acts as though the events at hand are what interest him, but I know that isn't true—I feel it.

As the next set of culverts are opened, water comes boiling up from the bottom of the empty chamber, frog free. The spectacular flow of water is pressed by gravity alone from Lake Gatun into the immense concrete chamber. The drama is overwhelming, and the canal, the locks, Federico against me, and the feeling that my life is being taken away with the flow of water make it hard to breathe.

I watch the display. Water in the last chamber rising slowly until it's finally even with the sea level outside, the huge gates splitting apart, wheeling slowly back into their niches in the walls.

The tug proceeds through the locks step by step, the tremendous basins swirling with churned water released by the subterranean culverts raising it to the next level. The crowd doesn't part or ease its press against us. We're forced against each other until the last gates open in the last lock and the tug steams out onto the surface of Gatun Lake.

There are cheers and movement toward the end of the lock and finally we're able to stand apart.

I take some deep breaths. Federico is watching the closing gates and the people, avoiding my eyes but not moving away.

"Nature didn't win after all," I say finally. A dry, impersonal comment.

He smiles faintly. "We'll see."

One Hundred and Seven

FOUR DAYS LATER.

Mother and I are packing clothing and small articles, leaving out what we'll need for a few more weeks. It's already October and I'm missing the opening of Oberlin, the orientation, the preliminaries to college life, but it doesn't matter. Certainly not to me and not to Mother, who believes the final days of construction and the opening of the canal are far more educational than the first days at any college.

"You'll have this for a lifetime," she says. (For the hundredth time.)

I've been present at the first lockage and at the removal of the last machinery. There's only the grand official opening left, and that's in ten more days. I'll see it.

I fold my clothes, the ones I'll be least likely to use again—jodhpurs and high-top shoes, just cleaned, maybe for the last time. Those early days with Harry were only three years ago. Impossible. It's a lifetime.

I'm walking toward the bed where the cases sit open and Mother is putting in a pair of patent pumps she's hardly worn when the first jolt hits.

It's hard and sharp as though the house has been hit by a giant club. Two small figurines fall off Mother's shelf and she looks at me perplexed. We don't say a word, just stand looking at each other, then I believe one of us says, "What in the world . . ." and the next jolt hits harder and it's not a single blow.

The house begins to jerk, side to side, hard and violent, and it doesn't stop. There is the noise of small items falling, Father's radio toppling, a heavy thumping sound, glasses hitting the kitchen floor, the entire contents of the cabinets flung onto the counter, a huge crash. Still it doesn't stop.

The force increases. The noise is multiplied by noise in neighbors' houses and the cries of alarm and dogs barking. Mother holds on to the windowsill and I hold the door handle, but the door keeps swinging and I'm almost flung to the floor. Then gradually, mercifully, the shaking begins to lessen and finally it stops.

Neither of us has screamed or cried out, but now with a tumble of words we rush downstairs:

"Good Lord . . ."

"Is it over?"

"Watch where you walk."

At the bottom of the steps the next violent shudder begins and it's more brutal than the others.

One Hundred and Eight

BOOKS FLY TO THE LIVING-ROOM FLOOR.

The breakfront tips over.

More glass shatters.

Rockers tumble on the porch.

There's more noise in the kitchen—flatware slithering and falling.

This time we both scream out as furniture slides by us and crashes into walls or against other furniture. Small articles are flung, skidding along the rug.

The earth is shaking, a haphazard, violent shaking, and we hold on to doorjambs and at one point to the kitchen sink until we can work our way outside, where we watch as it goes on and on, one violent attack after another. We don't dare go back in.

We cling to each other and call back and forth to our neighbors. It's surely the end of the world, the apocalypse, the colossal finish to everything—the canal, world trade, the earth and everybody on it. I must be weeping; I have tears on my face.

Mother and I hold on to each other and clutch a young sapling. Some waves are mild, others are more severe, but finally it stops. There's a shuddering ongoing in the ground, but the great attacks are over, it seems, and we cautiously venture back inside.

Electricity, water, and phones are out.

Father arrives, comes rushing up the steps.

"I'm not sure we should be inside," he says and huddles us together, and we've exchanged only a few words when it starts again and we rush out. It continues for an hour.

An hour, with only short breaks between attacks.

Having Father there comforts us but we're still helpless. There's no knowing when or if it will end. I'll write no essay on this. I'll never write again. I won't think of Federico. I'll do whatever I'm supposed to do, but *please make it stop!* I am afraid, really afraid.

God really doesn't want the canal completed. How big a sign does it take? I suddenly believe in a very angry Almighty, or want to, because maybe he could make this end. The relentless shaking, his punishment and reminder that there's no knowing or predicting much of anything, is clear and we've got it now. Doesn't he see that? Let it end, please. But it doesn't.

After a daylong hour, it finally seems to be over, really over. Minutes pass, then a quarter of an hour and another quarter of an hour, and we venture back inside.

We examine the damage: broken radios, crushed china, every conceivable kind of destruction to the strewn contents of our lives. We're destroyed in Dayton and destroyed now in Panama. We cling to one another, weeping.

One Hundred and Nine

THE NEXT DAY THE *RECORD* MANAGES AN EDITION in spite of damage to their presses. The needles of the Ancon seismograph were jolted off the paper, it says. Walls were cracked in Panama City, there were landslides in the interior, and a church was leveled before the hour ended. It's all we can think or talk about.

Canal construction has already been thoroughly examined, and it's announced that the locks and Gatun Dam are unharmed—there's no damage to any part of the work. I'm stunned. It's a triumph of engineering and execution.

Colonel Goethals notifies Washington. Washington sends congratulations. Nature has not prevailed. Nothing, not even acts of God, is on my side.

"I want to leave tomorrow," Mother says. It's too much for her.

An hour of total powerlessness is more than she's willing to risk again, and the word *aftershocks* is little comfort.

There's hurried packing, quick goodbyes to neighbors, phone calls, and two days later she's on the *Advance*.

I'm alone with no school and Father at work.

I'll leave in two weeks, after the official opening. Father will come home two months later.

They've begged him to stay permanently, offered him obscene amounts of money, but Mother's refused without expression or raised voice. He'll pack up everything that remains and be home by Christmas.

There's no slowing any of this. It's a rush toward the end with everything on schedule. The earthquake has made no difference.

The house is empty all day. Without school, I rattle around, read, take short walks.

Water is let into Culebra Cut through six huge drainpipes in the earth dike at Gamboa, leaving only the midsection of the canal to be filled. I read about it in the *Record,* talk about it with Father. I read *El Unico* and talk about that news with no one.

When the dike is blasted, the waterway will be open between the oceans, and that event, the final one, is now three days off.

Father's been eating at the Canal Club. Sometimes I join him, usually not. I prefer to snack at home.

One Hundred and Ten

COOL AIR SLIDES UP THE HILL AS EVENING FALLS. I approach Federico's cabin and I'm not sure what I'm doing.

I mount the steps and see him exactly as I saw him the first time with Harry: a foot propped against the chair beside him, book in hand, reading, intent, alone.

Everything looks the same. There's no earthquake damage and his life is like it was before I came into it. I wonder if he's achieved that in his mind, too, if I'm erased there. I don't think so. I don't want to think so.

I step to the screened door and he looks up.

"My books are going to be too heavy to take back—do you want them?"

"Come in," he says.

I go in feeling like the stranger I was that first time with Harry, nervous and jittery. Of course, he's calm and pleasant.

"Is your house all right?" he says.

"Yes, fine. We're all fine."

"Did it frighten you?"

I nod and smile.

"Me, too." Nice of him to say that.

Nice. Everything nice.

I want to say, *We made this cabin ours, didn't we? Burned it up . . . or down. Shouldn't we be talking about that?*

I'll never feel this way again, I'm pretty sure, and yet all he says is "Sit down." So I do and I say, "I want to travel as light as possible, so books have to be left behind. Would you like to have any of them?"

He doesn't seem to register what I'm saying. He's looking right into me. I fumble on, fill the air with self-conscious words. "I didn't bring sweets this time . . ."

That was wrong, meant to make him remember our erotic history, but it's inappropriate and I want to die on the spot and he saves me.

"I can't take the books," he says.

"Ah."

"I'll be leaving in a few months myself. Can't you give them to the school?"

"Sure. That's what I'll do."

Okay, that's done. An awkward silence.

I ask him, "Are they using you now? Are you working?"

"We're putting dynamite in Gamboa dike, tons of it. When it blows . . ." He shrugs.

That's right. Shrug. It'll be over. Some final work for you; I'll be gone. *Doesn't this bother you?*

He finishes the thought. "It will be all over. Oceans connected."

"The Spanish Church is going to be very angry," I say.

"I hope so," he says and smiles.

Not even a little anger at the Church. I hate it. We're so broken apart.

Our polite smiles fade. Mostly it's sad between us, even for him—I can see that. It's grim and awful, the last we'll have.

Finally I say, "Thanks." I don't know what for.

My voice is strong and I don't know where that comes from. I stand to leave. He takes my hand. (Now it's electric.) Half shake, half warm connection, very civilized. Then he lets go.

To the door and out and he comes down the steps with me. At the bottom he gives me a smile and a nod, and as though to a child he says, "It's all right."

No, it isn't. I am righteously furious at him. I could attack him, scream and call him names with tears spurting out of my eyes. I'd cover him with my tears if I could—that would do it. That would make me feel better.

He says it again: "It's really all right."

Am I a dog to be put to sleep? He comforts me as if he were my owner.

I calm down but feel the tears rising. I turn quickly and start walking.

Federico watches me leave for the last time. I'm wrecked and don't look back because I can't keep from crying and I don't want him to see my weakness. I hold my head high.

I want some dignity in the end.

THE SEVENTH WONDER
OF THE WORLD
One Hundred and Eleven

A NEWSPAPERMAN DREAMS UP THE IDEA: A signal relayed by telegraph wire from Washington to New York to Galveston to Panama. It will be almost instantaneous and President Wilson will press the button that opens the canal. Dramatic and plenty newsworthy.

People gather from all over the United States, from Europe and Asia, from all over the Zone. All of us board the labor train for Gamboa dike. Father has left in the early-morning hours to help prepare the auspicious event. I follow about noon.

It's my last trip rolling along the Panama Railroad Line and I have no feeling of nostalgia whatsoever. Not a trace of sentiment for those railcars I've ridden . . . how many times? Five times a week for 150 weeks. I do the math. Seven hundred and fifty? No. Have to double that—I ride twice a day. And the other trips to other parts of the canal. It's a big number. Sixteen hundred, maybe . . .

It means nothing. It's a train, that's all.

"'Scuse us . . ." School friends press close to look out the window. Their parents are staying on. They've started another school year. I'm not a part of them anymore.

We're pulling onto the Gamboa siding and we can see the dike with men still working there. The train comes to a halt and we tumble out and find places along the platform to watch.

Yards away the water of the lake laps at the dike's edge, ready to spill in. On the other side is the Cut, still empty, a vast space that's been filled with noise and activity and trains all these years. Now there's only broken dynamite boxes, some switch shanties, watchmen's shacks, and a few warped and twisted rails, all of it ready to join the underwater world.

A tall, rangy boy from school standing near me says to whoever can hear: "What if the water doesn't hold up the banks? Could be big ol' muddy mush by tonight. Ha-ha . . ."

But nobody laughs and several girls roll their eyes—this fellow is not the brightest porch light on the block.

Of course, it's true. At least, it's an outside possibility—mud, mush, failure. And Father and all the other bosses and everyone on the Commission know that and are worried—they know anything could happen.

They're all gathered, engineers and electrical men and rail men (Father) and shovelers and crane men, and there's joy and pride and anxiety thick in the air.

People are filling in the platform around me and I see Father with the others—bosses and engineers—all of them smiling, talking and animated.

Among the laborers now climbing out of the work area is

Federico in a red shirt. I spot him easily. He's wearing red for rebellion—that's no accident. He makes his way through the workers looking for a place to watch, and he talks to the men as he moves along. I've never seen him in a work situation before. He's the leader even there. Finally he finds a place and sits and looks out over the assembly.

He spots me right away.

He sees that I'm looking at him and raises an arm. Just raises it, no big salute.

I'm surprised at such a public gesture, but no one on either side of him could know who he's hailing, so it doesn't matter.

I raise my arm in response, just raise it like he did. Then I turn back to the activity. It's beginning.

One Hundred and Twelve

OUT IN THE LAKE THE OFFICIAL LAUNCH IS APPROACHING with the colonel and other Commission bigwigs. They don't look a bit worried. Colonel Gaillard stands straight and proud not far below us at the viewing stand with Father. Everyone is present and ready. Even this momentous occasion is well organized, no time wasted, ready to go on the dot—time is a crucial factor in this show.

Suddenly there's silence. No announcement to the crowd, just the approach of Goethals's launch—the signal it's about to happen. In moments the seas will be connected, and it strikes me that after the deaths, false starts, lives changed, homes removed, populations displaced, shipping lanes redrawn, this really is going to happen.

There's a hush and not a voice can be heard, not a child's cry or a dog's bark, except for the rasping whisper of the rangy, pessimistic student. "Here we go . . ."

A Commission officer with a stopwatch in hand makes an announcement:

"It is now two o'clock. In Washington, President Wilson is walking from the White House to an office in the Executive Building . . ."

Eyes on his watch, all of us breathless except for me—I'm serenely watching from a great distance, numbed by the awful finality of it. Seconds pass.

"It is now one minute past two and the president has pressed a button in the Executive Building. One more minute, ladies and gentlemen . . ." All eyes are glued on the man and his watch.

Dead, expectant calm, a parrot's call off somewhere, sixty seconds tick by, then he looks up and says: "Now!"

As precise as the plan itself, it starts: a low rumble, a dull, muffled boom, and then a triple column of dirt shoots high into the air at the center of the dike and falls gracefully like a fountain.

There are cheers and applause and shouting. Several hundred charges of dynamite have blasted open a hole more than a hundred feet wide and water is gushing from the lake into the Cut.

Hats fly high, the crowd roars with applause, and there's whistling. Water gushes and the bosses shake hands—Father and Colonel Gaillard and all the others are exuberant and relieved. Backs are slapped, hands are grasped in strong grips, and men are embracing with relief to see it, some of those strong male eyes moist. Mine are. It moves me, this grandeur. Or maybe it's something else.

The stately official launch with the colonel moves toward the dike's opening and the cheering continues.

I watch from my distant planet, and then suddenly something happens that brings me back and makes it all worthwhile. It has to please Federico, and I know Harry loves it.

From the brush come two nearly naked brown men carrying their *cayuca* over their heads. It happens quickly. The men drop their dugout into the foaming water and hop in. They make their way expertly along the surface, through the Cut, rushed by the flow. All eyes are on them, the first men to use the connected seas—Panamanian men, indigenous men, slicing through the continent in their hand-hewn log boat, the first men to do it. It makes me smile. Harry better be seeing this, and I search for Federico's face again but can't find him. He's nowhere in the crowd. I never see him again.

I watch the two brown men until they are no longer visible, well on their way to the Pacific. The pessimistic teenage naysayer beside me watches, too, envy in his eyes. And that's it, the moment I'll remember: the great flush of water and the indigenous men using the passage as they should and the crowd smiling at them and pleased to see it, and my teen passion eclipsed by all of it.

The great event has seized me. I've become one of Goethals's unstoppable Americans. We've split the continent in spite of the odds, the earthquake, a warning from the Church, death and all the rest of it, and it's done. The canal is built. The seas are connected.

I feel pride and I'm surprised. It's the last thing I expected to feel on this day, but there it is.

On top of my misery.

One Hundred and Thirteen

THE SIDES HOLD. It's not muddy sludge. It's an open passage that requires constant dredging, which they're prepared to do forever if necessary.

Self-propelled dump barges, tugs, a drill boat, and a crane boat are brought up through the locks, the first procession from the Pacific side passing through Miraflores and Pedro Miguel. The dredges take up positions in the Cut; barges shunt in and out, dumping mud in out-of-the-way corners of Gatun Lake. Flood-lights are installed and work goes on day and night.

Two months later an old French ladder dredge named the *Marmot* makes a cut that opens the channel enough for deep passage. The first complete passage, using the locks from ocean to ocean, takes place almost incidentally, part of the workday routine on January 7, 1914.

I'm in Oberlin on that day, deep in research on Spanish seventeenth-century art with new Oberlin friends, one of them a fellow so much like Harry that I can't resist liking him and his tales of life in Kentucky and squirrel hunting and reading Tolstoy in the woods.

Tolstoy. I've found a friend.

On that day in January, an old French crane boat, the *Alexandre La Valley*, just going about its work, comes down through the Pacific locks and out the other side without ceremony, without much attention of any kind, and papers carry the item. I notice it right away. They point out how appropriate it is that the first passage should be by a French vessel, however humble. The French did make the first brave effort at a canal.

Sometimes great countries have moments of great civility.

I'm studying for term exams, doing well, making friends, while in Panama thousands are being let go, hundreds of buildings disassembled or demolished.

Engineers are relocating to factories in New York and Detroit, where there are opportunities in the new automobile industry.

Families are packing to leave, and there are farewell parties somewhere along the line almost every night.

Ships from every country begin passing through the canal at ninety cents per cargo ton; I read about that, too. And the most impressive aspect, the papers say, "is the ease with which everything works as though the canal has always been there, ocean-going vessels passing through day and night."

Goethals is kept on as governor and he runs the operation smoothly.

Harry's long gone. We never hear from him again. When I think of him in class, I don't doubt he's tramping around the world, shaking his head at inequity, talking to the "small fellow" in each country and breaking bread with him, partaking of his life and learning his language, searching for another Ruby.

And of course there's always news of unrest in Spain. It's

heroic to go there and fight for the "small fellow," though the politics have become complex and I want—need—to talk to Harry about it.

I bet he seizes a rifle and goes. Maybe not. He's a wanderer, not a warrior. But Federico's there, no question about it. It's what he lives for.

Or dies for—I'll never know.

One Hundred and Fourteen

ALL THIS IS BEFORE I GRADUATE WITH HONORS.

Before I marry.

Buy a house.

Have two sons.

And my Panama diary is packed away.

It's not a thick book, the last entry so bitter and pained that I can hardly stand to look at it. But I don't throw it away. And occasionally, like now, clearing the attic and searching through the trunk, I find it and I'm not able to leave it alone.

A few cubic inches of space—I should just leave it there. But I pick it up and the last pages fall open.

Funny—I see the whole thing again just looking at those last paragraphs. Maybe it's not so funny.

November 1913. The last time I'll write here, I'm sure. Seven more days at sea and all I can do is sit on the deck and try not to cry and write. If Mother finds this in Dayton she'll be curious—she doesn't know I've kept it. She might even open it against her better judgment, although it breaks one of her strictest rules—privacy. But with no one else in the house, she might take a peek. She'll see a phrase, something shocking from a time when she thought everything was under control, her family's lives virtuous and unwavering in Panama. And she'll continue reading, horrified, and then fascinated by her horror and horrified by her fascination—deeper and deeper, not able to stop—like me with Federico. She'll read, listening for footsteps, but I'll be away at Oberlin and Father at work, so she'll be safe but guilty and completely drawn in. A long time will pass and finally she'll finish and sit on the side of my bed, shaken, wondering what to do.

But it's all over. There will be nothing she can do. To confront me she'd have to reveal she's pried into my private life. And my offense, which she's just discovered, would be passed and over with. She doesn't know that Federico is so large a part of me now that nothing else can come in, no one else, ever.

I'm writing and squeezing back tears because people are walking on the deck and I don't want them to see me sentimental and teary—I'm stronger and tougher than that. Federico's tomboy.

This much I know—the pain will go away. I know it. That's just common sense. But right now my heart hurts, my whole chest hurts—no wonder they call it heartbreak. My skin hurts to touch—it hurts when it's not touched. And that will go away; it has to. So will Mother if she finds this and reads it. She won't do anything to me; she won't even confront me. She'll close the diary and slip it back into my dresser drawer and sit there stunned. And things will go on as usual.

Cheerful Dayton. Orville no longer tinkering in the shop because he's making trips to Washington and Europe, which he doesn't enjoy—he's famous now and that's no fun for him. Me moving dreamlike until I get my wits back. Mother pretending she knows nothing of "soap foam sliding down his arms and chest to his legs in the dark," and each time I come home from Oberlin she'll introduce me to nice Dayton gentlemen, good-natured Methodist boys eager to know me better and wanting maybe to have me between crisp Dayton sheets, the kind meant for proper conjugal unions that produce good-natured children in sensible homes not too emotional in nature, with all things under control, no lush Panama foliage that can turn to a hot streak of desire in a heartbeat. No heavy floral scent in the Dayton air. We're a clearheaded people, anxieties suppressed and kept in order at any cost. There are always two or three unbalanced citizens around, but we're a sensible bunch and tolerate them well. I'll soon be back there, back home. And all this will pass. I come from good Kentucky and Missouri stock and know that. I've experienced it.

I know common sense will prevail and I'll be fine.

Close the book, Mother—it's all over.